The Mountains Are Calling

—

The Mountains Are Calling
Kate Cavett

2018

Copyright © 2018 by Holly K. Conrad

First Printing: 2017

ISBN 978-1-7323333-0-7

Holly K. Conrad
P.O. Box 30472
Knoxville, TN 37930

Cover Photograph from pexels.com

To Robin

You have been not just a best friend, but a source of sanity, confidence, support and sisterly advice.

Thank you.

Acknowledgements

I would like to thank my online friends for your support in this endeavor. Your candid conversations about online relationships—the happy times and the hard times—and your willingness to talk with me about your own personal experiences helped me put words on paper. This book would not have been possible without you.

❧ 1 ❧
I-40 Westbound

"The mountains are calling and I must go!"

The quote by John Muir was one that I spoke often and one that I understood well. There is something about the mountains that pulls at me, tugs at my soul with the promise of beauty and revitalization. I love the rocky ravines, the foggy mornings, and the trees spiraling upwards towards the sky. The mountains are my go-to place when life gets overwhelming and I need a break from it all.

Like now.

The interstate stretched out before me, an endless span of dark gray asphalt glistening in the early fall sunlight. The dotted white line dividing the lanes flashed like a beacon to my left, guiding me to my destination. Trees lined the roadway, their leaves still a dark green but there was the occasional rebel, showing off a stray gold or red leaf. My fingers tapped on the steering wheel as I drove, and I sang along with familiar songs from my favorite playlist and let my mood and thoughts shift with the music.

It was the last day of September, and I was heading west from Knoxville, Tennessee towards the

Ozarks to do my best to unplug from what had been a frenzied summer and reconnect with myself and the world around me. Having spent the last eight months feeling as if I were being pulled in twenty different directions at once, I put a halt to the endless work requests that piled up in my email and decided that for the whole month of October, I would be somewhere else.

Somewhere along the way, I had gotten lost in all the things that other people wanted me to be and not really working on being myself. It wasn't just work, I reminded myself, but personal venues, too. Expectations can take a lot out of a person, and there is a price for being competent. I had gotten tired of being taken for granted with my job and being made to feel guilty for saying "no" or for standing up for myself. But for at least a few (hopefully) serene and happy weeks I would be away from all of that, and the only thing that needed my attention was me.

There would be people and things that I would miss while I was away. Saturday mornings at the Farmer's Market and the friends that gathered once a month for Supper Club. I would miss my roleplaying and gaming friends—both online and off—and I would miss the pulse of being in a small city. I reminded myself that all those people and things would be waiting for me when I returned, and hopefully, I would be feeling renewed and more like myself.

So westward I went, heading to the Ozark Mountains. While I had visited the Great Smoky Mountains many times, I had never been to the Ozarks. I put the range as a destination I wanted to visit on my bucket list. Now, burned out and needing rejuvenation, it seemed like as good a time as any to go. I am a sucker for the great outdoors—even if I hadn't had the time to get out much lately.

A friend of mine, who used to live in the area, had a rental cabin in the Ozarks, and he was willing to let me have it at a discount for the month. He had retired a year ago and was now living on a boat in the Florida Keys. He said renting the cabin kept him in beer money. So, taking a deep breath and a large chunk of cash from my savings, I packed my car and headed west on a two-day drive into the mountains of northern Arkansas.

My plans for my stay in the Ozarks was simple: I would rest, relax, and finally get to start a writing project that I had been meaning to get to for the better part of a year. I would read some books I'd been meaning to read, and of course, spend time exploring the trails of the Ozark National Forest.

Soon, the tall stands of trees lining the interstate gave way to the city of Memphis and scores of businesses. I was almost sad to see the trees go, but I had been driving for quite some time and was ready for a break. The thought of Memphis barbecue and some blues had both my mouth and soul watering in anticipation. I checked into a chain hotel and chucked my travel bag on the floor beside the bed. I dug out my copy of Jack Kerouac's *Big Sur* from the bag, and headed out to Beale Street to find some food and music.

I went to a local place—there is no sense in eating at a chain barbeque joint in Memphis, or anywhere else for that matter—and was shown by the smiling host to my table for one. The interior of the restaurant was dark, and the smell of smoked meat filled the air. Strains of blues reached my ears as I followed the host through the restaurant and more than a few heads turned to watch me curiously as I made my way to my table.

I knew I was looking out of place in my blue monochrome skirt and purple Foo Fighter's concert shirt, but I didn't care. I was here to eat, not for unwanted opinions on my choice of travel clothing. One couple, who was sitting near me, continued to watch as I perused the menu. The man finally looked away, but the woman continued to look on, and I could not help but cringe a little at her scrutiny. You'd think that she hadn't seen many travelers. Or maybe my hair was sticking up in a funny way or I had toilet paper on the bottom of my shoe. (No, I didn't and yes, I checked.) I wasn't sure what accounted for her rudeness.

After stuffing myself full of good food and listening to music while pretending to read Kerouac's *Big Sur*, I returned to my hotel room and tossed the book on the bedside table. I sat on the bed and instead of turning on the television or going over the notes of the book I had planned to write while up in the mountains, I sat with my legs crossed under me and let my mind churn over thought after thought.

I thought about my friends, online and off. I had two distinct communities of friends. Those who lived in town with me that I would see at parties or go out to dinner with, and those I knew from my online communities through various games and forums. What little free time I had to spend with friends was divided up between these two groups, and it was becoming difficult to juggle the two.

The people I knew personally looked at me with concern when I told them that I would be gone for a few weeks. Some of them nodded, telling me that it looked like I needed an extended vacation. Perhaps I hadn't hidden my stress as well as I thought I had. The truth was that I wasn't happy and hadn't been for a long while.

Then there were the internet friends that I knew by their first names or online tags only. People who seemed both close and distant to me. Some I had known for many years. Some understood why I needed to go; others did not. A few people made me feel like I was selfish for taking an extended break, although they were quick to put their own needs before anyone else's. It made me think about distance and disconnections and whether I needed to let some of those friendships go. Why try to maintain something when the other person doesn't seem to care or have time for you?

I thought about missed opportunities and things that I wished I had been able to participate in but didn't have the time to do so. There was a time that I swore I wouldn't let regrets fill my life, but lately, they seemed to have crept in. In the past two years, I found myself missing out on kayak trips, gaming conventions, and wine nights because I was too busy with work or playing an online game to participate. I wondered, not for the first time, if taking the month off to resuscitate in the mountains was the best thing for me to do.

One thing was for certain: there was no internet at the cabin. I was going to be more or less unplugged from most of my friends. There would be no online games or forums, and any email or phone calls would have to be on my cell phone. I wasn't certain what my cell phone reception would be like either, and it was quite possible that while I was up at the cabin, I would not have service despite my friend's assurance to the contrary. It was a bit disconcerting to think that I might literally be falling off the face of the earth for the month.

My musings were abruptly cut short when my phone alerted me to a text message. It took me a moment to remember where I had set it down and after a few minutes, finally found it plugged in at the desk, its dark cover blending in with the desk mat.

The message was from Bane, an online friend. He and I spoke often, both in the game that we play together and outside of the game with texts and the occasional phone call. When I think of serendipity, I think of Bane. An ominous name, I know, but he really is a sweet person. He was checking in on my long day of driving and wanted to make certain I had made it to the hotel and was safe for the night. Very much like Bane.

I texted back, *Drive was long but pretty, in the hotel now. Thanks for checking in.*

To which, he immediately replied, *Good. I'll check in tomorrow night, too. You're supposed to arrive at the cabin then?*

Yes, I replied. And then, because I could not help myself, *Anything happening online?*

They have a raid going tonight, but I am not running, he replied. *I'll let you get some sleep. Have a good night.*

When morning came, I was back on the interstate, wrangling my way through rush hour traffic. It was currently at a standstill. Around me, people were looking anxious and agitated at the traffic, and for a moment, I smiled. Other than wanting to reach the cabin before nightfall (because driving up a steep mountain in the dark was not something I wanted to do), I didn't have to rush off to be someplace to meet with someone about something. That was a good feeling. Soon enough, the traffic thinned out, and the Mississippi River stretched out before me, long, wide, and lazy on its trip towards the Gulf of Mexico, and I crossed the bridge into Arkansas.

Once again, I plugged in my favorite playlist and let my mind wander as I drove. Thoughts flitted across my mind like little birds. They settled in for a few moments before they left. I thought about my boyfriend, and how I should text him when I got to the cabin. I ignored the little niggle of disappointment that I hadn't heard anything from him last night. I also ignored the fact that I hadn't sent him anything last night and that communication is a two-way road.

The miles sped by as the landscape changed from river scrub to farmland, and finally foothills as I approached my destination. I turned off the interstate and continued to head north on the state highway and found myself weaving through small towns that time seemed to have forgotten. They had quaint little downtowns with soda fountains, family-run restaurants, and tiny post offices. They also had a fair number of empty storefronts, their dingy windows peering sadly out at the street. Seeing the empty buildings reminded me that while they were a charming throwback to when Main Street was the heart of American business, time had definitely not forgotten these places. The nostalgic image of these little towns was quickly marred as I neared their edges and chain stores and strip malls and fast food chains popped up alongside the highway.

It was late afternoon as I wound my way up the mountain through a series of harrowing switchbacks, all of which seemed to wind around steep inclines. My fingers were white-knuckled on the steering wheel around several, and I would hold my breath hoping that I wouldn't meet another car head-on while going around the tight, blind curves. I was also hoping that my GPS was going to be reliable with the spotty cellular service and that I actually had the right address. I wasn't certain what I would do if my destination were a turnoff at the top of the mountain with no shelter in sight. But, neither my friend nor my GPS had led me astray, and I was turning into the driveway of the A-frame cabin that would be my home for the next few weeks.

I turned off the car, shutting off Nickleback's *Miss You*, which seemed like an appropriate anthem, in mid-song. Around me, there was nothing but trees. There other cabins up here, but they were hidden from my view, giving me a sense of being truly alone. I wasn't certain if I was happy or uneasy with the feeling.

The front porch creaked slightly as I stepped across it and opened the door. The cabin was small, with only a single bedroom, bathroom, living area, and kitchen, but it would suit me just fine. The floors were a knotted pine, and they had a few worn throw rugs covering them. The couch, side chair, and coffee table were relatively new, but the kitchen looked like it had been put in twenty years ago and never updated.

I crossed to the back deck which had a fantastic view of the opposite ridge. It was easy to picture myself out here in the mornings reclining in one of the Adirondack chairs with my cup of coffee to watch the fog lift from the ridge. And again, in the evenings with the hush of night and a sky filled with stars. I leaned against the railing and drew in a deep breath, relishing the clean mountain air.

"The mountains called and I came."

⊂8 2 80
Will o' the Wisps on the Deck

It was nearly ten thirty at night. I had managed to unpack most of my things, and now I was sitting on the back deck of the mountain cabin that would be my home for the next month. I parked myself in one of the Adirondack chairs, enjoying the quiet night air complete with chirping crickets and a few owls. Above the trees, I had a peek at the starry sky. The twinkling lights were bright and unimpeded by light pollution. The moon was barely a sliver in the sky, and there were a few hardy fireflies still about, winking in and out like little faeries.

Or will o' the wisps my whimsical mind thought. No... better it be faeries. I just got here and didn't want to be lured to my death by malicious little witchlights.

I admit that I have a fanciful imagination. It helps when I am writing stories and participating in roleplaying games. It also helps me lose myself in daydreams, or in this case, nightdreams, when the mood hits me. I could easily come up with some story to match this dark and starry night. Something perhaps with an unexpected romance and no malevolent little spirits seeking to draw people to their deaths.

It was dark. I mean, *dark*. I had turned the lights off in the cabin and could barely see the hand in front of my face. I had the feeling that it was a good thing that I was by myself because me stumbling back inside the unfamiliar cabin, groping about for a light switch while trying not to break a knee on the furniture, was not going to be a pretty sight. The only lights out here were from a smattering of cabins on the opposite ridge, and one peeking through the trees to my right. All signs telling me that I was not completely alone up here on the mountain. None of them did anything to illuminate the darkness that had settled around me or disturbed the sense of isolation.

I should have been in bed an hour ago, propped up against the pillows for a chapter or two in my current book (or in *Big Sur*, which I was trying to slog my way through) before turning off the light and drifting into dreamland. The long drive in from Tennessee and the nerve wracking climb up the mountain had taxed me both mentally and physically, but while I felt weary, I didn't feel sleepy. If I had been at home, I might have fired up my computer and reached out to some online friends, but without an internet connection, that was not a possibility.

I had been out here on the back deck for a few hours. First, in the wan light of early evening when the sun had fallen low enough that the mountains and their trees blocked the light. I had eaten supper out here at the small, round metal table that had been tucked away on one side of the long deck and had thought about how this would be perfect in the afternoons to have a glass of wine with some cheese and a few crackers. I had watched what little light had been left slowly turn to deep indigo and finally to near black. Now, I sat in the darkness, feeling the calm of the mountains seep into my weary body and regretted not picking up a bottle of wine in town before I made the steep drive up the mountain.

I wasn't long in the quiet darkness before I was struck with an odd sense of loneliness. Something that I both had and had not expected. I visited the Smoky Mountains many times in the past and have always enjoyed my trips, but they were always with friends. I had people to sit with out on the back deck, to share a glass of wine and conversation. It was just my first night, I reminded myself in an attempt to shake off the lonely feeling. I needed to get used to the quiet.

It was a beautiful night. One meant to be shared with someone, and somehow, my soul knew that. Someone not to fill the air with idle chat, but to look up at the night sky and marvel at the beauty that surrounded us. Someone to hold hands with and enjoy the romance of the night even if it doesn't turn intimately romantic.

Not ten minutes later, my phone on the table beside me chirped, telling me that I had a text message. I picked it up, the light from the screen marring the otherwise still night. I looked at the name and smiled, *Bane...* he was checking in, as promised, to make certain that I had made it up the mountain in one piece. Leave it to Bane to chime in when I was feeling lonely. He had an uncanny knack of reaching out to me when I needed it most.

Bane was always checking in with me when I was traveling or had some issue pop up. When my furnace went out, he either Skyped or emailed me every morning and every night to make certain I was alright. In his words, he wanted to make certain that I hadn't succumbed to hypothermia. He did the same when I traveled, checking in each night for a little while.

I typed a short message back telling him that the trip went well and that I was now sitting on the back deck enjoying the quiet night and relaxing in the cool mountain air. The reply was almost immediate: *I wish*

I could be there with you. I had to smile at that. We chatted back and forth for a while before he said goodnight, and I was left once again in the quiet of the night.

I sat there for a long moment in the darkness, thinking about Bane and how we had met online and gradually came to know one another. We were just friends. There was nothing romantic between us. In fact, he was dating someone, and I was happy for him.

Soon, my mind drifted to other people, including someone else that I had met online a few years back before I had met Bane, and grown very close to—closer than I had with anyone else. He became my Wonderwall—that one person online that you just click with and everything seems to fall into place. About a year and a half ago, he became my boyfriend, and we started an intimate online relationship. We've talked online, and over video chats, but have not spent time together in person. Sound strange, doesn't it? We live in different states, me in the east and him in the southwest, but the far reach of the internet made it possible for us to meet, get to know one another and start a relationship.

He went by the strange tag of Restless. Despite the name, he didn't seem restless about too much. He never delved into why he chose the name, and I never asked. At some level, I assumed he did so because he thought it was edgy—and available. He worked second shift and he did hate his job, though. When asked how his day or week had been going, he often replied "Eh, okay, I guess," or sometimes, "Terrible," so, in retrospect, I suppose that his choice of online tag fit him.

Restless had my cell phone number, but he didn't call or text often. Email or video chatting was his preferred method of communication with me when we were not playing an online game together. Email did make it easier to type out longer messages, to be sure, but while I was up here in the mountains without a WIFI connection, texting or calling was going to be easier. Although, I suppose if I had to, I could type out an email on my phone.

I hadn't sent him anything yesterday when I stopped for the night in Memphis, but I did send him a text about ten minutes after I arrived at the cabin. While I was originally dubious at what kind of cellular reception I would have up here, I had been assured by my friend in the Keys that I would have a signal and would be able to receive calls and texts and check my email on my phone. My phone told me that my text went through successfully, so I was confident that Restless had gotten it.

As that thought went through my mind, a part of me wondered if I would hear from him at all. As close as we were, I only heard from him on the days that we were supposed to get together online. Otherwise nada. I suppose that begs the question: how much of a Wonderwall was he really? Or for that matter, were we as close as I thought we were?

I love you, genuinely... that typed phrase came back to me one day after I had virtually cried on his shoulder about feeling taken for granted. He had given me every indication, through words and emotes, that we were indeed, close and he referred to me as his girlfriend to other people.

I checked my phone, half hoping that I had something, anything from him, but knowing that I didn't. It took several long minutes for the data to be downloaded and after a few seconds of checking for texts and scanning the few emails that had appeared on the screen, I closed the program. He hadn't sent me anything. I wasn't surprised, just disappointed.

I sat there for a long while, looking out towards the ridgeline in the dark and wished that I could talk to Restless. To share this evening with him, even if it would just be through typed messages. Emails and texts worked just fine when he was looking for it, but that always didn't seem to be the case. With a small twist of my lips, I typed up another short text to him about the nighttime view from the back deck of the cabin and how I wished he were here.

Nearly an hour later and with some reluctance to leave the near-perfect night, I hauled myself up out of the chair. I was feeling a little more than disenchanted. It was a feeling that had been steadily growing for the past few months.

I thought that I would feel relief once I got up here. A quiet sense of peace and hope, not a subtle depression that threatened to well up and drown me in melancholy. Maybe there *were* will 'o the wisps around, invisible and draining me of hope. Maybe, and more likely, the two-day drive here had caught up with me, and I needed to go to sleep.

Restless wasn't going to send anything back tonight. I imagined that he was busy with work. When he got home, he'd sit at his desk and play one of his many games. He'd get lost in an online world until the early hours of the morning and not think of his girlfriend up on a mountain in Arkansas. Or he might. Perhaps there would be something tomorrow, I thought with the same measure of hope that came with a bright, new day. I stretched and made my way back inside and managed to make my way to bed without stumbling over too much furniture.

⚛ 3 ⚛
Coffee in the Fog

Morning came bright and early. I was woken up not too long after six by birds chattering in the spruce tree that was near the bedroom window. At one time, 'not too long after six' was not a time that I wanted to be awake. Over the years, that had gradually—as in at a snail's pace—began to change. Now, getting up at five or five-thirty was normal for me. Six was sleeping in. There were times that I wondered when that unfortunate reality happened.

Truthfully, I didn't mind. There was a sense of accomplishment in getting up early and having most of my work out of the way by lunchtime. That allowed me to have meetings in the afternoon or, on a few days, have my afternoon free. It also permitted me to usually have Fridays off—something that I had little trouble in getting used to. Having Fridays off enabled me to be able to spend more time with Restless (online) and on occasion, Bane when he had the day off and Restless wasn't available.

I hadn't set up my coffee pot the previous night, so as I dug through the plastic tub that I had wrestled in from my car (emphasis on wrestle), I thought about my day and how I intended to spend a good chunk of my morning on the back deck enjoying the view. First, with my coffee and breakfast, second with my laptop, starting my personal writing project that I might or might not have the courage to send to a publisher or try to self-publish. Heck, if it was warm enough, I might spend my entire day on the back deck with the trees, birds, and ridgeline as company.

Being afraid to put my writing out for people to see was something that I needed to get over. After all, I wrote a lot of things online that other people read. I belonged to roleplaying guilds in a couple of MMOs that I had written extensively for, and no one had shamed me for what I had written. I wrote in an online roleplaying forum and had gotten favorable reviews from my writing partners. I had written tabletop roleplaying games for my local group that they seemed to enjoy and encouraged me to write more, so what did I have to lose?

After all, most of my teachers growing up thought that I would go into writing and when I choose a business degree followed by an MBA, they were surprised. At the time, a business degree seemed to be a more stable career choice than trying to be an author. While I loved to write, the chances of me being picked up and published seemed farfetched, and a job with a well-heeled company was offered up as I was handed my diploma. I took the job and contented myself with writing on the side. Then I went into business for myself as a project manager and organizer for hire, which seemed to fly in the face of having a stable career.

It took a lot of hustle to make my new venture work, and it stretched me beyond my comfort zone, but that was a good thing. It enabled me to reach out to my community and help organize events and draw people together. I could connect with people across the United States, and, on one lucky occasion, in England. I was doing well enough to take an extended break, although there would be a few bits and pieces that would need my attention while I was here. And being able to go to work in your pajamas is not overrated by any means.

It takes a lot of discipline to be self-employed, especially when your office is in your house. I play a few online games, and it is easy to jump into one and not get back out for several hours. Or all day. That had been a problem for a little while, but after a month of little income and late nights binge working as so not to miss a deadline, I learned to balance game time and work time. Telling someone that you didn't do what you were supposed to because you spent too much time playing *Guild Wars 2* isn't a good way to get paid. Or get a referral. Or a return client.

While the coffee brewed, I walked outside on the back deck and looked out over the ridge. The morning fog hung low over the trees, shrouding the vegetation underneath. I love the fog. It didn't invoke any creepy horror movie references for me but did impart a sense of serenity and beauty. There was something about it that drew me and spoke to me in sweet whispers. It was almost as if it were a magical world calling me home.

I walked back inside once I was fairly certain that the coffee had finished brewing and collected my e-reader and phone. *Big Sur* was on the nightstand beside the bed where I had left it last night, and I ignored the small voice telling me that I was determined to read it. I was struggling to get into the book. Once I had my cup of coffee in my hand (in a white ceramic mug with a picture of a bug-eyed dog on it), I was back on the deck in the Adirondack chair to enjoy the peaceful morning.

I wanted to leave my phone behind in the house, but old habits die hard. Or in this case, don't die at all. Being up here alone, my phone was my lifeline to home and friends. Besides, I told myself, I needed to check my email and texts, and, if last night were any indication, it would take a little while for them to download via cellular signal. It was an excuse. Another habit that I should break for few weeks, but I had spent so long checking it every fifteen minutes that it was ingrained.

There was nothing of importance this morning. Not that I had expected there would be. Still, I was disappointed that I hadn't heard from Restless. I suppose it wasn't that strange. Unless we had planned to meet on a particular day, I didn't hear from him. And if I sent him something on a day that we normally didn't get together, it was rare that he ever responded.

It hadn't always been this way. During the first few months of our relationship, we'd talked every day, usually online in the MMO we played together. He was responsive to emails and texts that I sent and sent a few himself. Gradually, that began to change. I can't put my finger on exactly when it happened, but a few months ago, I realized that he was more absent than he was available.

I sighed, feeling unhappy, and took a sip of my coffee as I gazed out at the fog. I could see the dark shape of the trees and small hints of fall foliage through the murky white. I breathed in the serenity of the foggy mountain morning, closed my eyes, and tried to exhale out my jumbled thoughts and quiet my mind. I failed in that endeavor.

It was something that I did not fully understand, no matter how hard I tried. If you cared that much about a person, wouldn't you try to check in? Wouldn't you respond to any e-mails or texts that were sent? Even Bane, who had a girlfriend he seemed serious about, cared enough about me to check in regularly and respond to anything that I sent him.

I had to wonder what happened to my relationship with Restless that we reached this point. How did we go from talking on a daily basis to me starved for just a simple acknowledgment from him? I used to feel like I was close to the center of his world and now I felt like I was hammering on the door, trying to get in. It really shouldn't be this way, I thought miserably.

I wallowed in self-doubt and pity for another ten minutes before I snapped my phone off, deciding that the more I dwelled on Restless, the more the beautiful morning would be spoiled for me. I marched the phone inside and set it on the kitchen counter and vowed that it would stay there until lunchtime. No emails. No texts. No worrying about whether he was going to contact me. No worrying about whether he was even thinking of me. I was going to eat my breakfast and read a chapter or two in my latest e-book and enjoy the morning before pulling out my laptop for some writing.

So, armed with my refilled coffee cup and a bowl of vanilla yogurt and fruit, I made my way back outside to where the fog and my e-reader waited and settled in to enjoy the rest of my morning.

As much as I would like to say I spent the rest of my morning in peaceful solitude while I read about someone else trying to unravel their own problems but getting caught up in the very things they were struggling to let go of, I found my thoughts wandering back to my Wonderwall and wondering why he couldn't find the two minutes it would take to check in on me.

With more chagrin than a person alone needed to have, I set my e-reader down with a sigh and retrieved my phone from the kitchen counter. The urge to see if I had anything from Restless won out over my willpower to push the thought out of my mind. It seemed that the hero in my book wasn't the only person struggling to let some things go.

○ 4 ◎
Whitaker Point Trail

I didn't get much work done in my first few days in the Ozarks. I suppose, in retrospect, I wasn't going to do much other than get a bearing on my surroundings and settle in. My expectations of spending a few easy hours clacking out the beginnings of a story on my laptop resulted in a few hours spent staring out at the distant ridgeline pondering one thought after another and only writing two paragraphs. Both of which were horrible and, I was fairly certain, unsalvageable even after a few pathetic attempts at editing.

The next two days were not better. My attempts to go for my daily walk didn't fare well as there were no sidewalks and little ground on either side of the narrow road before it sloped up into a steep hill or down into a steep ravine. The locals were not used to seeing pedestrians walking along the switchbacks, and that brought its own dangers.

One particularly harrowing moment came one morning when a large blue truck had zipped around a tight turn, the driver gunning the gas to spur the beast of a vehicle up the incline. A tree effectively shielded me from his view as he went into the switchback (something I realized all too late) and before he knew it, there I was on the edge of the road. I jumped towards the tree line on the ravine side of the road to avoid getting hit. The ground sloped steeply down, more than I had realized, and my attempt at escape only resulted in me sliding down six feet and coming to an abrupt halt at the base of a large and immovable sycamore. I am pleased to say that only my pride was hurt, although I would be sporting a few bruises by the end of the day.

As I lay there on the ground staring up at the yellow foliage and distinctive white bark of the sycamore, I thought about the Darwin Awards and how not to become a victim of natural selection due to your own stupidity or short-sightedness.

Just what had I been thinking to take a walk along the narrow road when I had a whole national forest filled with trails nearby? I vowed to go hiking on one of the trails next time I needed to clear my mind.

The driver of the truck did stop to check on me. He screeched to a halt with small pieces of gravel spitting out from under his tires. He hopped out of the monster of a truck and walked a few paces down the incline towards me. He was a linebacker of a man with the good looks of the congenial boy-next-door.

Once he saw that I was still alive, he was very apologetic for nearly running me over. He was also kind enough to give me a hand back up to the road. After assuring him that no damage was done and declining his offer to drive me back to the cabin, he drove off, and I made my way home.

The day after that mishap, I kept my vow that if I wanted to do any walking, I would do it in the national forest. I opened a map of the national forest I had picked up on my way in and looked at the various trailheads dotted about the area. So, after breakfast, I pulled on my hiking boots, slipped on a turquoise windbreaker, and made my way towards one of the Whitaker Point trailheads.

It was a twenty-minute drive from the cabin to where the Ozark National Forest began, and another five minutes to the trailhead. Two cars were parked in the pull-off which was big enough to accommodate six cars. The trailhead was marked with a wooden fence and a brown sign with the words, "Whitaker Point Trail, 5 miles". I didn't plan to walk all five miles today, but perhaps I would do so one day before I left.

I enjoy hiking. I love to get out into the peace and quiet of the forest and see all the wildflowers, mushroom and moss patches, and gaze up at the trees. I love to hear the birds, listen to the rush of a spring, and smell the fresh air. Out here I can clear my mind—and sometimes fill it back up again. Unfortunately, I didn't have the opportunity to hike often anymore. There were just too many demands on what little free time I had.

Today I knew that I would fill up my mind during my hike. That was, after all, a part of the reason why I had come to the Ozarks in the first place. An opportunity to rattle through my various thoughts without distraction or deadlines, and find some space to breathe. Find some space to remind myself who I was.

Introspection came easily as my legs moved along the dirt trail. With each breath, I imagined myself inhaling good energy while exhaling bad. I let my mind reach out to the trees around me and the ground beneath my feet, making a connection to my natural surroundings. The trail had a mild incline upwards, winding towards a ridge that would offer a picturesque view of the valley below, and I felt a little winded. I hoped that I would not regret my choice of trail tomorrow. At one time, such a hike would not have been a problem. Now, I wasn't so sure.

I spend a little time thinking over the work project that I had left when I came here. It wasn't yet finished but was in its final stages. My part was done, and I had left instructions with the project lead for finishing it out, including a checklist of things that still had to be done. She had assured me that all was well in hand and thanked me for my efforts.

I had another project coming up once I returned, but things would be slow moving on it until after the holidays. There wasn't anything on the docket after that until spring. That didn't bode too well for me, and I wondered if I needed to find some WIFI at a local coffee shop and look for a few new projects to bid on. After all, if I didn't work, I didn't get paid.

You'll be fine, I reminded myself. I'd been over my bank account and knew that I could take time off and still be okay to pay my rent and utilities, feed myself, and buy Christmas presents in December. I hadn't had a real vacation in nearly two years and I needed the time off to recover from the burn out that brought me here in the first place.

I nodded to an older couple who were on their way back down the trail. They each were wearing brightly colored windbreakers with Patagonia's logo sprawled across the upper right shoulder. Her sneakers were bright pink, and he carried a pair of walking poles. I often wondered if walking poles actually helped or just made the carrier look like a serious hiker. It was hard to tell. Both the man and woman greeted me with nods of their heads and cheerful hellos. Neither broke stride as they passed me.

When I grew old, I wanted to be like that couple. Able to get out and about to hike, shop, and spend time with friends. I didn't want to be someone who could no longer get out and enjoy life. That started with me now, I knew. I couldn't spend idle days on my couch watching television or sitting at my computer playing games. I had done a lot of that over the past few years, and it had started to take a toll on my body. My energy levels were down, and the few hikes that I had gone on were more strenuous than they should have been, even though I was used to going out for a walk once a day.

But walking once a day didn't do much for me since I was spending the rest of it on my rear. I needed to cut back on the amount of time I spent sitting, I told myself firmly. Cut back on the number of hours that I spent online. That could start while I was here, I decided. I could get out more, get my body used to being outdoors again and when I returned home, do my best to keep an active lifestyle. I could eat better too, cutting out soda and chips and forgoing my daily glass (or two) of wine in favor of just having it on special occasions. Both my budget and my liver would like that.

Not long after I passed the older couple, I reached the top of the ridge. The trail continued downwards, my assumption being that it was heading towards the other Whitaker Point trailhead. I took a seat on a boulder and looked out over the trees that were dotting the landscape below me. Most were still green, but some were turning to fall colors—yellow, orange, and red. I thought that in a few weeks the view would be breathtaking, and I made a mental note that I would come back to hike the entire trail and see the trees again before I left at the end of the month.

My mind turned back to the older couple that I had passed just a few minutes earlier. I wondered if they had hiked down to the other trailhead and back or if they had come to this spot and took a breather as they enjoyed the view and the quiet companionship of each other's company. I thought about all the shared memories that they must have and felt a twinge of jealousy.

I wrote a small story about them in my mind. I decided that they had been married for a long time. They had grown children, but perhaps not grandchildren yet. They lived in a tidy house and knew each other so well that they could finish each other's sentences. They knew how each other liked their coffee and gifts were now small, thoughtful things instead of grand gestures. I didn't know if any of that was true, but it sounded good.

I always thought that by this time in my life, I would be married. I was a year shy of thirty, and several my friends had already tied the knot. Me getting married was something that my parents had always assumed would happen. Something they had told me would happen. As my mother frequently pointed out: little girls grew up to get married and be mothers. It was a sign of my parents' upbringing when that was what was expected of little girls. I had thought so, too, but so far, hadn't met anyone that I thought I wanted to spend the rest of my life with. At one time, I wanted someone to move through life alongside me and make memories, but somewhere along the way just living life became more important than finding someone to marry. When did I stop wanting that? Had I stopped wanting it? I wasn't sure.

A piece of me was satisfied with my life and what I had. I was my own person with my own space. I liked where I was, and while I was comfortable in being in an online relationship, there were times that I missed having someone to go out to dinner with. Or go Christmas shopping, enjoy a festival, or—I thought of the older couple—take a hike in the woods. The only way I could spend time with Restless was to sit inside on my computer, and most of that was just typing, the occasional email, text, or time spent playing a game. I was complacent with it, I realized, and had been for over a year.

That realization sent a small surge of unease through my stomach when it hit me. I had been that person who would go hiking in the Smoky Mountains two or three times a month, ran two miles a day, and enjoyed the great outdoors. Now, I was spending more and more time of my free time on my computer and not as much getting out and doing other things that I enjoyed. That was probably why I had gained a few pounds and hadn't been able to lose them. I thought about my earlier vow of wanting to spend less time sitting and more time being active. That wouldn't jive too well with an online relationship that required me to be on my computer to spend time with my beau.

My lips pressed together as I thought about the growing sense of disconnection that I had been feeling towards Restless for the last few months. I knew its cause. It stemmed from all the times he said he'd get together with me, then failed to show. A few times, I had simply given up waiting for him and logged into a game, only to find that he was already there. Sometimes he said something to me, and sometimes he waited for me to say something to him. His go-to excuse was that he had lost track of time. More and more often, I wondered if there was a hint that I was missing.

I also realized that I didn't know how well he liked to do things that I liked—such as hiking, camping, festivals and community events. Vague comments like, "Sounds fun," were just that...vague. I would ask the next time I spoke with him.

Whenever that would be... was the glum thought that followed.

I shifted on the rock and tucked my hands into the pockets of my windbreaker. There was a lot I should talk to him about, I realized. Things that needed to be said for a long time and perhaps a chance to figure out what was happening in our relationship. Maybe if I opened the dialog with him, it would encourage him to do the same.

The wind ruffled my hair, pulled back in a ponytail for the hike, as I pulled out my cell phone and opened my email app. The urge to see if he had emailed me was overwhelming, and I gave in, feeling hopeful that by now there had to be something. The screen stared back at me while my phone tried in vain to pull a cellular signal up here and failed. I sighed and shut the phone off. I would check again when I got home.

I spent an indeterminate amount of time sitting on the rock wishing that he was here with me enjoying the view and wondering if he had yet responded to the message I sent a few days ago. Eventually, I hauled myself up and started back down the trail towards my car. I was hungry and didn't think to pack anything to eat. I purposefully turned my thoughts from Restless to a grilled ham and swiss sandwich as I made my way back the ridge.

Going back down the trail was easier than going up, as it was mostly downhill. I passed another couple, this one younger and holding hands and murmured a polite hello. Another ping of jealousy spiked in my gut, and I could easily imagine them, ten years later, reminiscing about a hike together along Whitaker Point one splendid fall afternoon.

I would like to say that I didn't dwell on that during my drive back to the cabin, but that would be a lie.

∽ 5 ∾
Laundromat WIFI

The next few days at the cabin were more productive than the first. The hike I had taken along Whitaker Point Trail had loosened up my mind, and I was able to get into a routine. After deleting my first feeble attempts at writing, I was able to come up with a few chapters that I was happy with and didn't sound like something from a bad romance novel—which was good. I wasn't trying to write a romance.

But as the days passed, so did my supply of clean clothing. The cabin, which mostly saw only long weekend guests, didn't have a washer or dryer. So, late one morning I packed up my dirty clothing and my laptop and headed down the mountain and into town.

My destination was a coin-operated laundromat I had passed on my way back to the cabin from Whitaker Point Trail. It was located in a dismal looking shopping center sandwiched between a mom and pop pizzeria and a money lending storefront outfitted with more neon than Las Vegas. Across the street was a coffee shop decorated in a retro's fifties theme, complete with a poodle skirt painted on the front window. A sign in the laundromat's window advertised free WIFI for patrons and from the glimpse that I had when I turned into the drive, had a few people inside going through the motions of doing their laundry.

I parked in the shopping center's lot and went to the pizzeria for lunch. It was dark inside, reminding me of the barbeque joint in Memphis, but without the smell of smoked meat. The deep walnut paneling and dark burgundy booths did little to help the stained-glass lamps hanging from the ceiling illuminate the interior. The sign by the front door said to seat yourself, so I made my way to a table for two and sat down. A pair of menus, printed in a plain, no-nonsense font on white letter-sized paper and shielded in plastic sleeves, were tucked between the wall and condiment tray. I picked up one and scanned it out of curiosity, finding that not only did this place have pizza, but an array of salads and pasta.

My waitress was a young woman who probably had graduated high school only a year or two earlier. Her hair was bleached blond and pulled back in a sloppy pony's tail. While she wasn't unattractive, the bored look on her face didn't do much to help her appearance. She had one pen tucked behind her ear and another in her hand, making me wonder if she'd forgotten the one behind her ear. I could smell the scent of some sweet-flavored vaping smoke on her.

She was patient, answering my questions about individual pizzas and salads and pointing out a lunch special on the menu—a piece of New York style pizza and a salad—that I had missed. I ordered a piece of pepperoni and a house salad and was promptly left as she walked back to the kitchen to put in my order.

While I waited for my food, I took the opportunity to look around the restaurant. It was small, probably only housing thirty people at a time. The walls were decorated with various memorabilia from the local high school and the University of Arkansas in Fayetteville, which was further to the west.

Several frames holding what appeared to be family photos were interspersed along the walls, creating a sense of belonging. I wondered if the family had deep roots here.

I didn't have deep roots in a small town. That was something reserved for cozy movies where the protagonist went back home to deal with crazy relatives and rekindle an old flame from high school. I had an old flame from high school, but he wasn't anyone that I'd be willing to rekindle anything with. In fact, the more that I think about the time when I had been dating him, the more embarrassed I got about. Harsh, I know. I think he ended up with a basketball scholarship somewhere.

I gazed up at the picture of a young boy proudly holding up fish he had caught. It was next to another picture of him in his teenage years, wearing a football uniform. The number twenty-eight was proudly displayed in white over the royal blue jersey. The first photo looked to be about twenty years old, and I wondered how old the boy in the photo was now. I guessed that he was now probably close to my age. Did he still live in this small mountain town or had he moved on to bigger pastures? Was he going to come home one day to his crazy relatives and rekindle an old flame?

There were only two other tables occupied in the restaurant. I wondered if that was because it was a weekday and early for lunch or if the place just wasn't that good. I couldn't remember too many other restaurants other than a Mexican place and a burger joint in town and hoped that I wasn't about to get a soggy, tasteless pizza with fake cheese and only two pieces of pepperoni adorning the surface. My concerns about the food and the restaurant's patronage proved to be unfounded. Half an hour later, the place had mostly filled up with chattering people on their lunch break, and I was finishing what had been a really good slice of pizza.

I paid my check, collected my laundry from the car, and made my way to the laundromat. The whole place smelled like Tide with a hint of stale water. The floors were black and white check, the surfaces of the tiles scuffed with age. The walls had been painted a soft yellow sometime in the distant past and were decorated with plastic signs giving various instructions about the machines. The whole place had a tired, depressed feeling despite the cheerful color on the walls, but at least they had WIFI.

I claimed a pair of machines and dumped my laundry in. One machine started without issue. The other not so much. It took some doing to get one of the machines to take the coins. No matter how I tried to jiggle and coax the quarters on the slide into the slot on the machine, they refused to go. As I struggled, I began to have visions of me diving into the machine to fish out my clothing to transfer to another machine. That was not going to be a pretty sight. After several failed attempts, a tired-looking middle-aged woman with a two-year-old on her hip showed me how to jimmy the level so it would go in properly.

As my laundry churned in the machines, I disobeyed the sign that read, "DO NOT LEAVE YOUR LAUNDRY UNATTENDED! PEOPLE WILL STEAL IT! NOT RESPONSIBLE FOR STOLEN ITEMS!" and went across the street to the coffee shop. The sign warning people not to leave their laundry had been posted in multiple places in the laundromat, and I wondered just how big of a problem stolen laundry was. I didn't have any idea.

I returned a few minutes later, a large latte in hand and laptop case on my shoulder, to find my clothing still chugging away in the machines, and not purloined by any laundry thieves. I sipped my latte as my laptop fired up and pondered if anyone would be tempted to steal my laundry. Was my clothing interesting enough to be coveted by someone? Sure, I had cute underwear, but how desperate or low would you have to be to snitch someone's t-shirt?

I know that I had planned to more or less unplug and stay unplugged from the internet for the month, but the free WIFI (heck, any WIFI connection) was too hard to resist. I was going to be here for a few hours anyway, so why not take advantage of it? I ignored all the warnings that I had heard about internet addiction and signed onto the WIFI using the posted guest password. The writing I told myself that I would do could wait.

The first thing I did was open my email. Since I hadn't opened it on my laptop for several days, it took a while for it to load. Most of it was various junk solicitations that I would delete. Some were from Amazon telling me about a book that I might like to read (and they are usually right), and some were work-related. I deleted everything from before today. I had already filtered through those on my cell phone (although my laptop made it so much easier).

I crossed my legs under me on the hard, wooden bench that was situated against the large front window and twisted my lips into a small moue as I pondered whether I wanted to send an email to Restless. He had, after two days, finally responded to that first message I sent. His response of, "Great! Glad your safe!" was not quite the length of discourse that I had been hoping for. I let pass the use of 'your' instead of 'you're,' although I did think that Bane would have caught the mistake.

I had written Restless back, talking a little about my trip here and the scary switchbacks on the mountain, but didn't get a response and hadn't heard from him since. Bane, on the other hand, had texted at least once a day and was quite happy that I hadn't hurt myself when I slid off the bank into a tree to avoid being hit by the truck. He told me to stay off the road and stick to the hiking trails.

Feeling a little lonely, maybe from seeing the two couples on my solo hike along Whitaker Point Trail or maybe just from being, you know, alone, I decided that I would at least try to reach out to Restless. I wouldn't hear from him unless I at least made the effort. I checked the time and decided that he was probably awake, and wrote out a new email to him: *Good morning sleepy head! I managed to find a WIFI connection at a laundromat. How was work last night?*

I hit send and turned my attention to my writing project, adding another page before it occurred to me that I should check the washing machines to see if the loads were done. A testy looking man with a crew cut standing with a large basket overflowing with clothes in his hands was looking at machines with such a pinched expression that I figured that they might be done, and he was antsy to get a machine open. I can't say that I blamed him.

I tucked the laptop back into its bag and slung it over my shoulder. I didn't think anyone would take it, but I wasn't going to risk it. I couldn't afford to replace it and I really, really needed it for work. Not to mention my writing project and notes were on it.

Peering around the man, I could see that my machines still had ten minutes left on each one. So, I did an about face and marched back to the bench, but not before I heard the man's sour remark of rude people taking up all the machines. I pretended not to hear and went back to my bench, pulled out my laptop again, and checked my email.

I felt my heart leap when I saw one from Restless: *hugs and holds tight* Work wasn't too terrible for once. Are you enjoying your time in the mountains?*

I quickly typed up a response: *I am enjoying it. Wish you could be here though. Glad that work wasn't too bad. Do you have plans for the day? *rests head against shoulder**

I hit send as Crew Cut Guy gave up trying to intimate the machines into washing faster and took a seat on a hard orange plastic chair. He dropped his basket on the floor, causing some of the clothing to topple out. I could see his lips moving in some sort of curse as he picked up his wayward clothing. I pulled my writing project back up and had only typed two paragraphs before my email trilled telling me that I had mail.

I opened Restless's response: *leans head against yours and rocks back and forth* I wish I was there, too. Not much in the way of plans, today. You?

I replied: Just laundry this afternoon and a bit of writing. I plan to spend this evening on the back deck enjoying the crickets and trees. *snuggles close*

His response came a few minutes later: *strokes hair* That sounds like a perfect evening. Wish I could share it with you.

I typed back: If you were not working tonight, we could spend the evening together. Although my phone might give up the ghost trying to send a volley of emails from the cabin.

It was a few minutes before he responded: I wish I didn't have to work either, but I have bills to pay. So, you said you are doing laundry, what does that leave you wearing?

I stifled a laugh and typed back: Nothing so sultry. Just jeans and a t-shirt. I am at a laundromat that has WIFI, so I thought I'd see if you were up.

His reply was quick this time: Laundromat? Well, there goes my idea of fun in the laundry room. As for being up, I am always up when you are around.

It was exchanges like this that I liked. Conversation between us flowed naturally and was dotted with small emoted gestures of affection and flirtation. Restless was affectionate, and he always made me smile. Talking with him made me forget all the frustrations I had when he wasn't responsive.

I was smiling when I went to pull my laundry from the machines, stoically ignoring Crew Cut Guy who made another remark about people taking up all the machines. I dumped my clothing in a pair of dryers, both of which took my quarters without issue. As I settled back on the bench to continue my email conversation with Restless, I saw Crew Cut Guy take not only the two machines that I had vacated but a third one that someone had emptied.

I guess the one machine rule didn't apply to him.

༺ 6 ༻
Stormy Afternoon

The next morning, the fog on the ridge was thicker than usual. Dense tendrils of the stuff curled lovingly around the trees, blanketing their branches like spectral Spanish moss and shrouding their trunks. The sky above me was thick with dark clouds. What had been a series of bright mornings with lovely spots of sunshine speckling the redwood deck, had turned rather dreary and dark. I wondered if a thunderstorm was rolling in.

I sat on the back deck and sipped my first cup of coffee, feeling quite chipper despite cool and gloomy morning. Talking with Restless always boosted my spirits and our two-hour long conversation via email while I sat at the laundromat had definitely perked me up. We had even ended with plans to chat again this afternoon via texts. It would probably more than just chatting. That was something I was feeling quite optimistic about.

This morning brought both a drop in temperature and an increase in wind. Long chilly drafts blew across the deck and swept up the leaves that had fallen into tidy little piles against the cabin.

The leaves still held their fall colors of red, gold, and orange, and the colorful piles made me think of a child's art project. Deciding that it was a too cold without the sun shining to work on the back deck, I went inside to eat breakfast and tackle some editing in my writing project.

I poured myself another cup of coffee as my laptop booted up and settled in at the rectangular dining table to work. I easily lost myself in editing my story, working through each paragraph and adding little bits of embellishments. I tidied things up and corrected a few sentences and added some missed words. When I was finished, I was both pleased with the chapter and feeling like a disciplined writer.

My half cup of coffee had long gotten cold, so I took the opportunity to stretch and have a break. I dumped the rest of the mug's contents down the drain and washed the cup by hand, and then did the rest of my breakfast dishes. The cabin did have a dishwasher, but since it was only me, it was just easier to wash things by hand. I sat back down twenty minutes later and started on the next chapter to be edited.

By the time I stopped for lunch, and to check my phone to see if Restless had woken up, I could hear thunder in the distance. I turned on the television and consulted the channel guide tucked in next to the cable box to find a weather station. With the difficulty that always seems to come to me when operating a television remote that I wasn't familiar with, I managed to find a weather report. It was not a pretty process. There is nothing like a foreign remote control to make one feel completely inept. I would have storms all afternoon and, though there would be a break in the early evening, more were coming tonight.

I shut off the television, picked up my phone, and checked my texts, finding that Restless had gotten up early, went to the bank, and now eating Thai food from his favorite take-out place. That man ate more Thai food than anyone else I knew. I texted him back, asking about how his evening was, how it was pouring buckets of rain here, and how I wished he had enough vacation time to join me in the Ozarks. I went to fix a sandwich for lunch while I waited for his reply.

Two hours later, the rain was coming down hard while thunder bounced off the ridge and seemed to echo through the valley. I stood at the sliding glass doors overlooking the back deck and watched the raindrops hit the wooden slats and jump back up, creating tiny little showers. The wind was hard enough to bend the trees, making their tall trunks sway back and forth in the storm. The leaves that had been blown into small piles this morning were now wet and strewn haphazardly across the wooden slats of the deck.

Restless still hadn't replied to the text I had sent at noon. I tried and failed, to stamp out my disappointment. I was certain he'd found his way into an online game and was too absorbed in it to think to check back. I wanted to be stoic about it, after all, the man was allowed to have hobbies, but if he had planned to get online, why did he tell me that we'd spend time together today? Or if he had been asked to do something by someone else, couldn't he have at least told me the change in plans, so I wasn't sitting here waiting for him to reply? It was, I reminded myself, par for the course.

I went back to my writing, and for another hour or so, managed to pull my thoughts together enough to finish out the chapter that I had been working on. Still, it had been hard, as my thoughts keep moving back to Restless and why he couldn't at least send something back saying that he'd ended up with other plans. That was only polite, right?

Maybe I was just expecting too much.

I didn't want to be one of those people who hovered over their significant other and demand all their free time. As was often the case when I was waiting for a reply from Restless and not getting one, I spent a lot of time getting myself upset over the lack of communication. If I couldn't make a planned get-together, I told him. Couldn't he do the same? But, did that make me someone who hovered? Couldn't I just roll with it and accept that sometimes things happened?

But they seemed to happen all the time, and never once did he ever message me to say he wouldn't make it. I, at least, would tell him when my plans changed, and I couldn't meet him. He never returned the favor. He just left me wondering.

The cold brought by the rain was seeping into the cabin, and I found myself uncomfortably chilled. I put on a pot of coffee and slipped on a hoodie to help ward the cold off. I leaned against the kitchen counter, watching the coffee brew in the small pot and brooded over the lack of communication that always seemed to accompany Restless. It seemed our relationship went from a happy high to a bottomed-out low all the time, and I was getting tired of feeling like I was on a rollercoaster.

My phone chirped while the coffee maker made the half-gurgle, half-hissing noise that comes when it is finished brewing. My heart leaped with some vain hope that it might be Restless. I looked at my phone to see that I had a text from Bane.

Hey you! Just checking in for today! He had written. *You're probably writing, text me when you can!*

Taking a small break, I texted back. *Aren't you supposed to be working?*

I poured myself a cup of coffee and added cream while my reply chugged its way through. The storm didn't seem to be helping the tenuous cellular connection. I leaned back against the counter and waited for the reply to come—which I knew it would. Bane always replied.

I will reiterate here: Bane and I are friends, good friends, but just friends. We played an online game together and often paired up to level characters, or run dungeons. We talked quite a bit out of game, too. First, it was just once or twice a week as we communicated changes in plans. Then, it grew to more and more as our friendship grew. Over the past few months, I had spent more time talking to him than Restless.

I am at work, but taking a break, too. Long afternoon filled with meetings needs coffee. Lots and lots of coffee. Did you do anything exciting today?

Just worked on the book. No hiking since it is pouring rain. Was supposed to talk to my boyfriend this afternoon, but... shrug. I didn't have to explain more than that. Bane would know exactly what I was talking about.

Not a usual day for the two of you to get together, is it? Came through a minute later.

I let out a sigh and took a sip of my coffee. *No, but we talked yesterday and decided to spend today together too. But, he is AWOL doing something else.*

Did he at least tell you he was going to be busy?

That was the difference between Bane and Restless. If Bane couldn't get together when he said he would, he'd tell me. He told me when he needed to leave a conversation and didn't leave me hanging, wondering if he was going to send something back. He was infinitely more reliable than Restless. If Bane could spare two minutes to send me a message about a change of plans, Restless should be able to, too.

Nope. Just a message asking about my day this morning. I sent one back asking about his evening at work was, but... nothing. I typed back.

I know you hate that, he replied. *Need to talk about it some? I can give you a call.*

I frowned at my phone. I was feeling tired and sad, like an old, faded dishcloth that had been left hanging on a laundry line in the rain. Wet, wrung out, and not important enough to be fetched from its soggy fate. The hard edge of the counter pressed against my back and the smell of freshly brewed coffee reached my nose as I read the text several times. Bane shouldn't be the one who had to jolly me out of a sullen mood, I thought with some bitterness, Restless should. But, Restless often was the cause for me to feel morose.

All I had to do was say yes, and in a few seconds, my phone would ring, and Bane's soothing voice would be on the other end, ready to help me re-establish my self-worth and challenge my reasons for staying with someone who routinely made me feel like Plan B.

I don't want to eat up your time at work. I typed back. I didn't want him to get in trouble for making a personal call. However, as soon as I hit the send button, I knew that I was also stalling. I didn't want to face the fact that Restless and the distance that was growing between us was something that I needed to think over while out here in the Ozarks.

I don't have to be back in a meeting for another fifteen minutes. It isn't much time, but if you want to hear a friendly voice, I am here.

Thunder rolled softly in the distance while the rain continued to come down. I could hear it hitting the roof of the cabin, the sound soothing and pleasing. I liked thunderstorms. I would curl up with a cup of coffee and a good book on my couch and let the patter of rain relax my mind. There was something oddly romantic about a thunderstorm in the mountains. Once again, I wished that I wasn't alone.

My fingers hovered over the phone for another second before I typed back, *I'd love to talk.*

⋐ 7 ⋑
Picnic with Kerouac

It was mid-week, and I was feeling cagey inside the cabin. I hadn't gone anywhere for the past three days, having been content to sit and write and enjoy the ridge. However, today was a different matter as a mild case of cabin fever hit and I found it difficult to focus on my book. After spending a good twenty minutes prowling restlessly inside the cabin, I decided that I was long past overdue to get outside.

I managed to pound out a few more chapters in my writing project, although I was putting off the task of editing my raw writing. I had promised myself that I would do that today. But as the morning passed with me mostly looking out over the ridgeline with my thoughts wandering again over various subjects, I realized that I wouldn't be able to focus on editing anything until I had an opportunity to clear my head.

The last time this happened, a hike had allowed me to sort through my various musings and gotten me to the point where I could focus again, so I decided that an afternoon spent walking along one of the many trails of the Ozark National Forest was just the thing I needed. Only this time, I would pack something to eat.

After lunch, I pulled on my hiking boots, put on my turquoise windbreaker, and after shoving some food, water, and the copy of Kerouac's *Big Sur* that I had been slowly making my way through into a backpack, I climbed in my car and worked my way down the mountain. I was getting a little better at not wincing and gritting my teeth at every switchback, but it was still a little scary. I vowed to have my brakes checked when I got back to Tennessee.

This time, I drove to the Redding Recreation area. They had a campground and picnic area there close to the Mulberry River and had access to several hiking trails.

The drive through the Ozark National Forest was scenic and soothing, although I could imagine on the weekends the winding roads might be gridlocked with visitors seeking to soak in the fall foliage. I didn't know when peak season occurred here. However, I knew it had to be soon.

The storm from Monday had swept through, drenching everything in a great deluge with its passing. A fair number of leaves had been shaken off the trees and the rains scrubbed the mountain air from clean to pristine.

The rains that had soaked the area had mostly dried up. There were still spots of mud in the forest, and no doubt on any hiking trails, but I could deal with a little mud. I just needed to remember to pull my hiking boots off when I got back to the cabin.

I did not do much hiking in the full flush of fall. Back home when I still had time to hike, I would hit the trails in the Smoky Mountains, but once the leaves began to turn, I put up my hiking boots. When the peak hit each fall, the trees would turn to brilliant colors and be absolutely beautiful, but the hour-long drive to the park could stretch to as long as three or four hours—and one year, it went to six—with the crush of people bent on visiting. Instead of battling the hordes of visitors who came to spend a not-so-quiet fall day in the Smoky Mountains, I usually waited until the spring when there were fewer people.

There were several campers set up in the campground when I arrived. I imagined that there might be more rolling in come Friday as people sought a weekend getaway in the park. I felt a small twinge of envy as I looked at the RVs set up. I enjoy camping and used to go twice a year with my friends. Once in the early fall and once in the spring, although we usually went to state parks. I thought that it would be fun to get an RV and tour the country, staying in state and national parks as I wound my way from one coast to the other. It was another item on my bucket list, but not one that I was confident that I would ever get to. I'd want someone to travel with and right now, I felt like my prospects of finding a traveling partner were dismal.

The sun was shining brightly, its rays causing the waters of the Mulberry River rushing past the picnic site to sparkle like someone had cast glitter over its surface. Big fluffy clouds filled the sky, and as I breathed in the fresh air and took in the subtle symphony of nature, I felt my cabin fever melt away.

I headed towards the trailhead, thinking that I could get a mile or two hike in before returning to the picnic area to eat my snack. I took a loop that worked its way up and over a ridge and then back around. Once again, I let my mind flow freely as I walked and enjoyed the great outdoors and was surprised when my mind decided to settle on my writing project, flushing out little details in the current chapter that I was writing.

As I wound my way back around the loop, my mind went to the next chapter in my project, and I worked through scene ideas and dialogue that would progress the plot. I waved at an older couple with a dog who I passed on the trail. A small sense of jealously cured inside me at the sight of them enjoying the day together, but instead of jumping to my own relationship questions, my mind stayed settled on my book.

My hike finished, I sat at a picnic table, its rough surface gray with weather and age. A slightly faded memo penned in black Sharpie notified me that Julia and Joshua were here and in love three months ago. I have never taken a Sharpie to anything to announce that I was in a relationship with someone. I could imagine Julia and Joshua sitting here one bright and sunny afternoon and scrawling the little love token on the table before leaving. I put Julia and Joshua out of my mind in favor for food and immersion in my book. I pulled *Big Sur* out of my backpack and I managed to lose myself in the book and stayed that way for nearly forty minutes.

Kerouac had written the novel in 1962, recounting trips he had taken to a cabin in Bixby Canyon not too far outside of San Francisco. I had first heard of the book my junior year of college in passing from a friend who had to read it as part of a contemporary American Literature class. I can't remember much about her opinion of the book, other than the comment of how messed up the main character had been. I wasn't sure if that was a reflection of Kerouac himself or a sign of the times where beatnik writers wrote emotionally strange and tangled tales.

I hadn't thought of the book until a few years ago when I heard the song, *Bixby Canyon Bridge* by Death Cab for Cutie. I was a few years older and wanted to feel like a well-read adult, so I bought a copy of *Big Sur* with the intent that I would read it and feel accomplished. It ended up sitting on my bookshelf for nearly two years before I plucked it off and stowed it in my suitcase when I packed for this trip. So much for being an accomplished adult.

In the novel, Kerouac's protagonist, Duluoz, is battling his personal demons while drowning in alcohol. His trips to Bixby Canyon were an effort to find refuge from a life that seemed out of control, as he battled with the spotlight of sudden fame—which was as far as I had gotten in the book. Feeling as if one's life was out of control was something that I could relate to, although unlike Kerouac's Duluoz, I wasn't battling alcoholism. Small blessings, right?

I remember being told by my friend who had read the book for her American Literature class, the protagonist in *Big Sur* was a literary personification of Kerouac himself. I had to wonder how much of the book was fiction and how much of it was him recounting actual events, thoughts, and feelings. Kerouac had been an alcoholic, and if I remembered correctly, had died due to complications of long-term alcohol abuse.

The song by Death Cab for Cutie was hauntingly familiar to the book, perhaps because someone in the band resonated with the book's author. I wasn't certain of what ghosts were haunting the person in the song, but they had come to Bixby Canyon to commune with Kerouac's spirit. His hope in finding answers through some metaphysical means was met with silence. He berates himself for thinking that it would be different, that he would be given some sign from Kerouac's spirit. Finally, with the setting sun, he ends up leaving the area with no answers.

I wondered if that was going to be the fate of the character in the book. To strive to find peace and hope and some truth in his life and not being able to. A piece of that resonated with me as I could understand wanting to find answers to important life questions—such as relationships, aspirations, and faith—and being terribly confused as to what was the truth of these things were for me. It was a little terrifying to think that you could be the force behind your own destruction.

I took a deep breath and told myself that my situation wasn't anything like the protagonist in *Big Sur*. Whatever path I was on I wasn't going to end up in the same place as Duluoz. Yes, I had questions about choices I had made and needed to get away from the crush of normal life for a while, but the sense of disquiet that had been growing wasn't going to cripple me. I wasn't being crushed under the weight of popularity and dysfunction that had stifled the already suffering Duluoz. I just needed to find the source of what was making me unhappy and dig it out at the root.

Which might be easier said than done.

Like me, Duluoz was not happy. I could tell that he was depending upon other people to bring joy to his life. It was not working out for him, as relying on other people to make you happy never does. I wasn't certain what the root of my unhappiness was, but I hoped with time up here away from everything and everyone, I could figure it out.

I shut the book and set it down on the table next to the Sharpie marker proclamation. I wondered if Julia and Joshua were still in love or if there had been a falling out. As cute and endearing vandalizing a picnic table, a tree, or bathroom stall with declarations of love between two people might seem at the time, it was not a guarantee of success. That thought stayed with me as I ate my granola bar and grapes and I absently focused on the water rippling past me.

I thought about the older couple I had passed while hiking towards Whitaker Ridge and wondered how long they had been married. I knew that relationships took work, communication, and commitment. Whatever it took to stay in love and make a marriage work, they had seemed to have found it. I wondered if I might ever be that lucky.

In *Big Sur*, Duluoz finds himself in an affair with a friend's mistress. I wasn't certain how that love triangle would turn out, or how his friend would take the news when he found out. I wondered if the affair would be the salvation of Duluoz or the final nail in his coffin. This was the first Kerouac book I had read, so I didn't know if the author favored happy endings or if he left his book's main character broken and beaten and metaphorically bleeding, meant to be a warning to others.

I looked down at the book, thinking that no matter how unhappy I had been, my life was nowhere near as complicated or twisted as Duluoz's. Things could be far worse for me and whatever problems that I had paled in comparison to the problems of other people. I suppose that I should have been cheered by the notion, but instead, I sank into a calm, comfortable melancholy that stayed with me for the rest of the day.

☙ 8 ❧
Greetings from Tennessee

I found it amazing at how quickly time seemed to be passing while I was in the Ozarks. It is remarkable what a routine can do. I spent my mornings writing and couple of afternoons a week hiking along one of the many trails. A part of me fantasized about becoming a full-time writer up here in the mountains. Life would be much like it was now: foggy mornings with hot coffee and a few pages rattled out on the keyboard. I'd be both famous for my literary works and for being a hermit hiding away in a cabin, shunning human contact.

Yeah, no.

While I have no problem with being alone, I do like people. I like going out with my friends to movies and restaurants and, I thought with a glance at the growing pile on laundry on my bedroom floor, I like having a washer and dryer in my house.

As much as I didn't want to think about work while I was up here, it kept creeping up on me. Like today, I got a call from a headhunter who'd come across my name from a convention that I helped organize for the past two years. On the one hand, I was a little pleased that my name had come up and someone was interested in talking to me about a job offer. On the other hand, I wasn't certain if I wanted to go back to regular nine to five job for someone else. Still, I didn't have anything to lose by calling and talking to a potential employer but my time, and time was all I had while I was up here on the mountain.

So, the next morning, I found myself in a parking lot in town, on the phone with a group in Nashville, talking about the various projects that I had done over the past two years while working for myself and my work experience before that. I also had the horrible question of what I thought was my greatest strength and what I thought was my greatest weakness. I have no idea what they intended to do with the information, except use it in my annual employee review. Then there was the question as to why I opted to go into business for myself. Unlike the question about my weaknesses and strengths, explaining my choice to make the leap and be my own boss was easy.

I had spent my first few years out of college working first for one company doing general marketing materials and then a second company, in which I got my project management certification. I was attending a project management conference, something that was required for me to maintain my certification as a project manager when I realized that project management was an underutilized field. I had been talking with a small business owner who had a project to expand a line of products and make them available for marketing on the internet, but she didn't have any idea of how to go about it. She was attending the conference, at great expense to her, to figure that out, but still had a lot of questions. Long story short (too late?) she ended up hiring me to work on her project.

It had been long hours with little sleep, but she paid me well and referred me to another small business owner. The next year, she came back with another project. Soon, I had more requests for help than I had time to do it in and after some quick number crunching, I realized that I could make more money on my own than I could at my current job. So, I made the leap to become my own boss.

I liked making my own hours, going to work in my pajamas, and not having a yearly review where I'd be told that my raise and cost of living increase was a whopping 2.5%. I liked the freedom that came with being my own boss, although more than once I had to give up a weekend because I helped organize a convention or street fair. But, in the end, taking that leap had been well worth it.

One thing that I needed to manage better was my workflow. In the beginning, things had been lean, and I had to carefully manage my money. Then, like a dam overflowing and bursting in a flash flood, everything just seemed to take off. I ended up swamped with jobs and burning the midnight oil to get them done. The money was good—I no longer chewing my nails over whether I'd be able to pay my mortgage and keep the lights on, but I had little time for a social life. I found myself choosing between my in-town friends or my online friends, and if I spent too much time with one, the other would get pouty and drop hints about how I am never around.

That put me right where I was now. In the mountains recovering from a serious case of burn out. Hey, it could be worse. I, of course, didn't tell the prospective employer in Nashville that.

I rang off my phone call with the promise that I would send them my resume over the weekend. That necessitated another visit to the laundromat, but my pile of dirty clothes had been growing. I figured that I could get my laundry done and maybe (hopefully) connect with Restless. I could maybe get a little more work done on my book, too.

My book was coming along with far more ease than I thought it would.   The story had been in my head for a while now. It started first as a "wouldn't this be a neat idea," to character concepts and pieces of a plot. Slowly, bit by bit and a few pages of scattered notes later, I decided that I had nothing to lose to try to pull it together into a book. It took some time to organize my notes and come up with an outline. I spent most of last fall on that little task, slipping it in early in the mornings or late in the evenings. I finished it back in February but didn't have any time to work on it until I came to the Ozarks.

I felt a little like some famous but reclusive author who sought out destinations to write a book. Except that I wasn't famous. Or reclusive. Or an author. At least I had a destination. Not for any sort of muse for my book, which had nothing to do with the Ozark mountains. So, I wasn't anything like a famous but reclusive author, but a girl could have her little delusions, couldn't she?

It was getting to be late afternoon and I was back at the cabin. While the weather was reasonably cool, it was not too cold to spend a little time outside. I made myself a mug of herbal tea and headed out to the back deck to think about the job offer from Nashville and muddle through my thoughts on what I thought I might like to do. I settled myself down in my Adirondack chair to make a list of pros and cons with the pad of paper and pen I brought out with me.

I was back up and inside again within a matter of a few seconds because I managed to grab a pen that didn't work. I tossed it in the trashcan (why keep a nonworking pen?) and grabbed another one while I wondered if the nonworking pen was an omen. I had a friend back home with an entire drawer of nonworking pens. Every time one stopped working, she tossed it into that drawer. The rest of us could not understand it. Was she thinking that one day they would all start working again?

Back outside, I settled back into my chair, took a sip of tea, tested that the pen actually worked, and started my list. Pros for Nashville included a steady paycheck, steady hours, and not an up and down schedule that seemed to be the norm for working for myself. I would have my weekends free and paid vacation time. There would also be an employer health insurance plan, which was bound to be less expensive than the single person plan I was on now. In the end, I imagined that it would be less stressful and fewer hours of work since I would not have to go out and drum up business. Cons included having a boss, employee reviews, and giving up the business that I had worked hard to build.

And it would mean that I would have to move to Nashville. Don't get me wrong, I like Nashville. I do. I've spent my fair share of time in Music City U.S.A. I've trolled Second Avenue and saw a band in the historic Ryman Auditorium. It is just that I like Knoxville better. Nicknamed the Scruffy City, Knoxville has a funky, upbeat charm that resonates with me. I love the farmer's market, the myriad of festivals, and the growing number of local, chef-owned, farm-to-table restaurants.

Of course, with the spectacular view of the ridge, I soon found my mind wandering off the subject of the job in Nashville and moving onto other things. For a few minutes, I tried to wrestle my head back on the subject of the prospective job, but each time I tasked myself with my pros and cons lists, my mind ended up wandering off.

I decided to let it. I set aside the pen and paper and thoughts about Nashville. In the end, I wouldn't have to make the decision to leave until I got a job offer and I wasn't guaranteed to get one. I had also come to the Ozarks to sort through my thoughts, make some decisions about my current job, and hopefully recover from the case of burnout that had been on my back like a rabid little monkey since mid-summer, so I let my thoughts flow.

It was a beautiful night. The sky was clear, and the moon was a bright wedge of silver against an inky backdrop. The trees were tall sentinels off the deck, illuminated by the light that I had turned on to be able to write my list. I stepped inside to refill my mug of herbal tea and turn off the light to better appreciate the starry sky. I shrugged on a sweatshirt to help ward off the evening chill and, armed with my refilled mug, headed back outside to enjoy the night.

There were no fireflies tonight. It was far too cold for them now. I thought whimsically of will o' the wisps and faeries and all the other fanciful thoughts that I had had my first night here. I missed the little flashing lights dancing around the trees and thought that if I had managed to make it here over the summer, I would still be seeing them.

We have synchronous fireflies in the Smoky Mountains. My friends and I went to see them for a few years, traipsing with hundreds of other people with our folding chairs and spending a few hours in the warm June night watching the little beetles. Before a couple living in the Elkmont area announced that there were synchronous fireflies in Tennessee and they watched them every year from their front porch, the only place that synchronous fireflies were supposed to exist were in the mangrove forests of southeast Asia. Soon after they made the announcement, other people stepped forward. Now, there are many places in North America where you can go and enjoy the unique light show, ranging from Pennsylvania to South Carolina, and all the way to Arizona.

It had been a few years since I had gone to see the fireflies as things had just gotten too busy. I still had friends that went, and each year they would send out an email invite. Maybe I would go with them this June if I could find the time. Or maybe, I needed to realize that how I spend my time was often a choice. I would have had plenty of time to go with friends to see the fireflies if I hadn't been so intent on getting online and playing a game.

The weight of loneliness settled over my shoulders like a thick blanket. It would be nice to have a friend here to share the lovely night with me. Not for the first time, I wished that I had thought to invite someone to come with me. But, all my friends worked regular jobs and taking off for a month-long vacation was not something they would be able to do. But, I realized a moment later, that I didn't have to be completely alone. I had my cell phone and a sketchy cellular signal. I could reach out to someone.

I texted a friend of mine from home, asking how things were with her and within five minutes, she had responded. She ended up calling me after a few texts, and we spent the next twenty minutes talking on the phone about everything and nothing. The weak signal dropped the call on us twice, but we managed to get connected again. The call had both eased and sweetly plucked the pangs of loneliness that I had felt, and I spent the rest of evening feeling quietly content.

It wasn't until much later, when I was brushing my teeth before bed that I realized that the urge to check for any emails or texts from Restless hadn't hit me. Not once during the entire evening had I scooped up my phone and desperately checked to see if there had been any word from him. I smiled at my reflection, feeling as if I had shrugged off an invisible chain, if only for one evening.

It was a baby step, but I would take it.

‹∞ 9 ∞›
Weekend Visit with Karma

The greatest of life's plans come with big expectations and the idea of how everything will just fall into place like a children's puzzle of a pink unicorn prancing across a rainbow. You make plans, confirm them, and proceed with gathering the bits and pieces you need to execute it. You check and double check to make certain that everything is in order and go along your merry way blissfully unaware that something will rise up like a fetid and haggard undead corpse causing everything to fall apart over the short course of an hour or two. The undead corpse banishing the aforementioned rainbow and then eating the unicorn after the poor, hapless creature crashes to the earth and breaks all its legs.

Too melodramatic?

Maybe so, but that was my day so far and it didn't seem like it would be much better.

It was Friday. My texts to my boyfriend, Restless, had been flowing with ease and I was cheerfully optimistic because of them. We started in the morning around nine o'clock with a conversation about our weekend plans.

*Good morning sleepyhead! *gives a hug* Did you have a good night at work?* I had written him, wondering if he'd message me back or not. I wasn't expecting anything from him until close to noon, which was generally the time that he woke up, so I was surprised when ten minutes later, his reply came through.

hugs and holds tight work was meh... but not as bad as it could have been. Happy it is Friday and I have only one more night this week before the weekend.*

Weekends are good. Are you doing anything special? I figured that he was going to spend it online like he usually did. *Have you been to bed at all?*

A few minutes later another message came through, *No sleep yet. I have some errands to run but other than that, nothing special is going on. How about you? *runs fingers through hair**

I was sitting in the Adirondack chair on the back porch with my laptop and the remains of my cup of coffee. I set the laptop aside and curled my legs under me in the chair. *leans against* I am just going to write, read a little bit, and probably take a hike.*

brushes lips against yours Mm, sounds like a good weekend. Any room for me?*

I smiled, thinking this felt like the closeness that we had back when we first got together. Back when we were talking on a regular schedule and making every effort to keep it that way. *I could make some room for you, love. *nibbles on your lips**

We should take some time this weekend together, he replied. *Although, I don't suppose you have access to a chat room or Skype? *brushes lips softly against yours**

Not unless I go to the laundromat.

No... not there! Might get thrown out for indecent exposure!

My lips quirked in another smile, *You plan for me to be indecently exposed?*

His reply was quick, *I do... perhaps we could practice now.*

The rest of the texts quickly became intimate, and for the next three hours, I was snug in the little world that we created for ourselves. He signed off citing the need for sleep, and I didn't argue. Working nights, he sometimes stayed up through the mornings after coming home and then sleeping for several hours in the afternoon. What he did leave me with was the promise that he'd message me once he got up Saturday morning... and he wanted breakfast.

We had breakfast together often, or at least we spoke about it. We'd talk about what we'd make and then talk about feeding it each other. Eventually, the nibbling bits of egg, French toast, and bacon would become the nibbling of each other. The rest is easy to figure out. More than once after such an exchange, I would wonder what it would be like if he were actually there sitting across from me eating rather than just talking about it over Skype or a chat forum.

His mentioning of breakfast made me realize that my food stores were low, and I probably should make the harrowing trip down the mountain to the grocery store. I should have bought more food, I realized, but my habit was to buy a week at a time. I was only five minutes from a grocery store at home, and it was easy to get to. Here, it was a twenty-minute trip down the mountain praying at every switchback that I would not meet an oncoming car.

So, sitting down at my kitchen table, I made a grocery list while I mentally made plans for my weekend. Breakfast with Restless tomorrow, then he could get a few hours of sleep. Afterward, we would trade messages the rest of the day and maybe have a dinner "date." It seemed like a sound plan in my mind.

The first problem in the form of a work email came while I was still mulling over my grocery list. One of the projects that I had worked on and thought that I had left nice and tidy to finish out with the lead organizer had not finished and now was overdue. With a sigh, I made a note to call the lead organizer to find out what was happening and what, if anything, I'd be able to do about it here in the Ozarks. The call would have to wait until I got off the mountain and into an area with better cellular reception.

My trip down the mountain didn't fare too well. I was almost side-swiped by a large black SUV who didn't believe in the need to share a two-lane road. I might have been more forgiving of my car nearly pitching off the side of the road into a ravine had we been on a switchback, but we weren't. It was a rare section of straight road that didn't have too much of an incline. The truck drove on, either oblivious to the near-accident that it had almost caused or was too ashamed or afraid to stop because they knew they almost caused a wreck.

Getting off the mountain in one piece was only my first challenge. I hit both the red lights heading into town and then the two that were in the town, which now just seemed par for the course. I let out a sigh and wondered if I had done something to offend karma and had kismet turned against me. I know I shouldn't get upset over things like hitting multiple red lights in a row, but that just irks me. To no end.

Finally, I pulled into a parking space at the grocery store and pulled out my phone to call on the wayward project. It was half an hour before I got off the phone. Half an hour of finger pointing and snide accusations and me being made to feel miserable because I was on vacation in the Ozarks rather than at my home office where I could just hop in my car, drive ten minutes down the road and fix the problems that reared their ugly heads because the project lead hadn't done her job. Visions of getting another job with that company vanished with an unpleasant sense of disappointment.

Already, I could feel my weekend of writing and virtually snuggling with my boyfriend slipping away because I had to deal with a work emergency. A work emergency that should not even exist because I handed everything to the lead organizer in a nice little package two weeks before I left. I could imagine trying to juggle cozy messages with Restless and professional responses and advice with the people left on the project. I didn't see it working out too well.

I sat in my car for another five minutes taking deep breaths and reminding myself that I had done my job and it wasn't my fault someone else had dropped the ball. It wouldn't take up all my weekend to fix. Maybe I could get most of it done Saturday morning while Restless was still asleep and mop up anything left while he ran his errands after breakfast. When I had finally calmed down and felt that my cheeks were no longer red, I went into the grocery store.

What should have been an easy shopping trip turned out to be difficult, too. There was no thick-cut bacon, so I settled for regular cut. I don't like it as well, but I could manage. They had had a run on baked beans, leaving only a brand that I detested, so I decided to forgo my idea of baked beans with my grilled burgers and wondered if they had corn on the cob. And speaking of hamburger, all they had left was very expensive organic grass-fed beef that was going to cost me twice as much as I would normally pay.

There thankfully were not too many other people in the store today, but what few there were all seemed to pile up on me as I made my way down the aisles. I even made it a point to turn around and head to another part of the store when I found a clog of shopping carts, but even that didn't last too long. It was like I had a homing beacon in my cart drawing all other shoppers to it like honey draws bears.

One customer was particularly impatient. I had heard her made several comments about people being slow while they scanned the shelves for the items that they were looking for. I was apparently the straw that broke the camel's back when I was looking over the meager selection of cheese that they had, trying to decide if I wanted a block of aged cheddar or a wedge of brie. She came up behind me, huffed, and snarled out something about people hogging the case. I tossed the wedge of cheddar in my cart, gave her a dark look, and left.

And so, it went. I felt like I had negotiated a peace treaty by the time I left the small, rural market.

My shopping completed, I made it back up the mountain without meeting anyone coming down. I suppose that between my heart-gripping trip down the mountain, the terrible phone call, and my struggle through the market, whatever penance I needed to serve the fates had been satisfied.

The rest of my afternoon was spent working via my cell phone to email various people about the breakdown in the project and where they were now. It occurred to me as I watched my poor phone spend five minutes trying to send a pair of emails across the weak cellular signal that I might have taken my laptop and laundry with me down the mountain and used the laundromat's WIFI to figure out what went wrong on the project and get some clothes clean and send off my resume to Nashville.

I just couldn't win!

However, I had Saturday afternoon to look forward to. I was going to spend it via email and text with Restless and not worry about the project for a few hours. I went to bed with that thought in my head and woke up the next morning feeling rested and excited about my upcoming 'breakfast.'

I cooked some bacon and French toast and sent a text to Restless telling him that I was awake, and breakfast was ready. I nibbled a bit while I waited for him to reply. And nibbled some more and some more.

One cup of coffee and an empty plate later, I let out a small sigh and rose to clean up the dishes. Another three hours passed and the only emails I had were from Amazon and the two people I emailed about the project. I let out another sigh, wondering if he was still sound asleep. I picked up my phone and headed to the back porch. I might as well do some work untangling the knot in the project while I waited for him to wake up.

The morning passed to afternoon, and afternoon to evening. The only messages that I received were from the people working the project and Bane.

I managed to get the knot in the project untangled. The problem, it seemed, was that the lead planner had decided to quit didn't tell anyone until nothing happened and people started asking questions. When reminded that she was under contract to finish the project and was going to take a penalty in pay, she started to scramble to make it up and was going to blame me in an effort to not make herself look like an incompetent nincompoop. By seven that night, someone else had stepped up and taken the lead, and I had promised to email him my notes and checklist on the project Monday. At least they knew where the blame lay.

With yet another sigh—this one filled with disappointment—I resigned myself to the fact that Restless and I were not going to spend any time together today. It seemed like the perfect cap to what had been a lousy weekend in general. I went inside to fix a lonely supper and wished that things were different.

❧ 10 ❧
Dinner with a Sasquatch

The next day dawned with the soft drizzle of rain, a distant rumble of thunder, and fog thicker than pea soup. My plans to head down to town this morning, do some laundry, and hopefully talk to Restless would be put on hold until the fog cleared and the rain stopped. I was not going to navigate my way down slippery switchbacks when I couldn't even the see the road, let alone oncoming cars. I didn't want to test if fate had forgiven me for whatever transgressions had angered it Friday.

I took my morning coffee in the living room instead of the back deck. Even after my breakfast and shower, the rain and fog were still persistent. Feeling less than optimistic about my chances to get to town this morning without ending up at the bottom of a ravine, I booted up my laptop and lost myself in writing my book for the next few hours. It was still raining when I stopped for lunch, but at least the fog was gone. After some consideration, and a check of the weather channel, I decided to wait until later this afternoon to head into town after the rain was supposed to clear. I wouldn't be able to spend much if any, time with Restless, but at least I would make it down the mountain alive.

The laundromat wasn't too full when I finally made it there late in the afternoon. There was a young man, despite the chill of mid-October in the mountains, wearing a pair of boxer shorts and a faded t-shirt that advertised some band I'd never heard of. He was sitting in one of the hard, plastic chairs listening to something on his phone through a pair of blue headphones. His leg bobbled up in down in what I assumed was in time with his music. Or maybe it was just excess energy. His leg *was* jackrabbiting pretty fast.

The other occupant was an older woman whose gray-streaked brown hair was pulled back in a severe bun at the nape of her neck. She had the look of a rough life about her; her face was pinched in an unhappy expression, accentuating the lines on her prematurely wrinkled face. A pair of dark skinny jeans hugged her curvy hips and a trendy red and black flannel provided an incongruous match to her face and hair. It was like someone had spliced two pictures together from a magazine for a surrealist art collage.

I settled in on the same wooden bench I'd parked myself on when I first visited the laundromat and first sent off my resume to the company in Nashville. Next, I shot a text to Restless telling him that I would love to chat if he had some time before work. Two hours later, I had not heard back from him, but my clothes were clean and mostly dry. I had folded them neatly and stowed them in the back of my car. Hungry and ready for dinner, I made my way across the parking lot to the pizzeria.

Unlike my previous foray there, this time it was crowded when I entered. All the tables were full, and there was a group of people crowded in the small waiting area. The sign that once read "Seat Yourself" now said "Please Wait to be Seated." There more people were trying to stuff themselves into the small space after me, and I felt a little like a sardine. I was told by a chipper hostess with a chic haircut and a wrist covered in jingling bangles that I could either wait forty minutes for a table or take a seat at the bar immediately. I chose the bar.

No sooner had I sat down at the bar when a guy sat down next to me. He was a bear of a man, with long brown hair that was pulled back in a pony's tail and a bushy beard worthy of any lumberjack. He was wearing dark jeans, hiking boots, and a t-shirt that read *Going Squatching.* He pulled off a baseball cap that had a silhouette of Bigfoot adorning the front and rested it on his knee. I had precisely seven seconds to wonder if my choice to sit at the bar was going to be something that I would lament before he turned to me with a cheerful greeting and introduced himself.

I smiled politely, returned the greeting, and looked down at my menu with the hope that he would see that as a sign that I was not in the mood for conversation. I decided to go for a small pie and take the leftovers home for dinner tomorrow night.

"So, are you from around here?"

I looked back at the man next to me, whom I had dubbed Harry (for obvious reasons… too unkind?). His name was actually Desmond, which to me was as incongruous as the older woman in the red flannel and skinny jeans from the laundromat. I decided that he did not look like a Desmond, so Harry it was.

"Actually, no, I'm not. I'm here on vacation, doing some hiking and whatnot," I replied.

"Hiking? Really? Maybe you could give me some advice," he brightened. I wondered if he had ever met a stranger. "I'm heading out tonight to do a little squatching and would like to know some good trails. Do you know of any that intersect with some ridgelines?"

"Squatching?" I repeated. I had no idea what he was talking about.

"Yeah," he nodded, "going out and looking for proof of Bigfoot. You know, get some recordings of howls and doing some knocks to see if I get a response."

"Seriously?" I paused for a moment to give my order to the overworked bartender and looked back at Harry. I wondered if it were wise to invite conversation with him, but I had never met anyone who actively went out in search of Bigfoot.

"I take it you are not a believer?" Harry said after he had placed his order.

"Well, I've never really thought about it."

"I didn't believe for a long time, but I was coming back from hiking one late day and saw one, clear as day," Harry turned in his chair to face me. "Bigger than anything I'd ever seen and it sure as hell wasn't a bear. Smelled terrible and made the hair raise on the back of my neck. We stared at each other for a good fifteen seconds, before it grunted and took off through the woods. On two legs." He walked two fingers across the bar top in demonstration.

"Wow, must have been scary." For all my hiking, I'd never come across anything that I would remotely even consider a Sasquatch. A few bears yes, and more squirrels, rabbits, and chipmunks than I could count, but no bipedal apes.

I wasn't sure if I believed in Bigfoot, but if I had to give an answer then and there, I would have to say no. But that was okay. It seemed that Harry had more than enough belief for the both of us. And, also for the guy sitting on the other side of him who kept sneaking derisive looks at him from over his huge mug o' beer. He obviously didn't believe in Bigfoot, either. Harry didn't pay the man any attention. I couldn't say if Harry hadn't noticed his snarky leers or was just used to ignoring people who made fun of his belief.

"Scariest thing I've ever seen," he nodded as the bartender plunked down a bottle of beer in from of him. Unlike Mug O' Beer Man next to him who was guzzling a cheap lite beer, Harry had ordered a craft brew. "But, it made me a believer. That was about ten years back, not long after I was out of college."

"What did you study?" I found myself interested despite my initial reaction. You know what they say about judging a book by its cover. I only hoped that I would not regret opening this particular cover.

"Biology," he replied. I could see that.

"And you've been hunting for proof of Bigfoot ever since?"

"Just for the past three years or so. I worked a few odd jobs in St. Louis before getting a job with the Missouri Wildlife Resource Agency. I didn't have much time to get out and look for Squatch. Didn't even know where to begin. And, to be honest, I had to wonder if I really wanted to head back out find another one."

I nodded, turning my attention to my glass of water while I thought about that. Harry had a point. I wouldn't know to begin to look for Sasquatch. I wasn't sure if I would want to run into one.

"But, there are Bigfoot groups out there, and while working for the Wildlife Resource Agency, I came across one that seemed credible and not a bunch of kooks."

Mug O' Beer Man snorted at that, and this time, Harry turned to give him a dark look. Since Harry, even sitting, was close to four inches taller than Mug O' Beer Man, outweighed him by at least twenty pounds of muscle, and looked a little like a Sasquatch himself, Mug quickly looked away.

"Anyway," Harry turned back to me, eager to wax on about his hobby, "I got in with them and learned the ropes. I'm here as a scout for the weekend and thought I'd go out and look around before it got too dark. Never squatch alone."

"Not walking around in the woods alone at night does seem like sound advice," I agreed as our pizzas came. I was a little confused about his comment about not going out alone. It seemed like he was going to do just that.

I learned more about Sasquatch in the next thirty minutes than I could shake a stick at. Harry's enthusiasm for the subject was boundless, and his faith that he would eventually get some proof of its existence was admiring. Here is a guy that went out in high hopes of catching proof of a creature that most people didn't think existed and each time he came back empty handed, he didn't stop. He just made plans for the next outing and got right back out there. There is something to be said for tenacity.

He even played for me a few sound bites of Sasquatch calls that he had gotten in a previous outing. The long, low, and mournful cries didn't sound like anything that I had ever heard while out walking around in the woods (not at night, that's a good way to turn your ankle) and must have been spine-chilling to hear. The cries sounded out of place in the crowded restaurant, and more than a few people turned their heads as the mournful sounds drifted over the din of conversation.

Harry also told me about the negative reactions he'd gotten when people found out that he had seen Bigfoot. I hadn't expected him to get so candid about the ridicule he'd received from a lot of people for his hobby. He talked about having his truck painted with rude words and that he'd lost track of the number of times people had called him 'f'ing crazy' right to his face. That bit did come late in the meal, and he'd had more than a few beers to loosen his tongue by that point.

"You just have got to get a thick skin when people make fun of you," he shrugged philosophically. "There are other believers out there, and I've connected with them. A lot of people have seen Bigfoot, and many haven't said a word about it for fear that people will think they are crazy, but trust me, when you've seen one, there is no mistaking what it is."

It was later than I would have liked for it to have been by the time I left the restaurant, but despite my earlier reservations, I had enjoyed talking with Harry. I climbed into my car feeling pleased with how my evening had turned out and made the drive back up to the cabin. It was now more hair-raising than usual since it was dusk, and I had to rely on my car's headlamps to see the road. Dusk was the time, according to Harry, that Sasquatch would wake up and start their nightly foraging. I didn't spend much time searching the sides of the road for Bigfoot, though. I kept my eyes glued to the road. I didn't want to drive off the mountain and die.

Once back at the cabin, I couldn't resist heading out on the back deck and spending a few moments in the chilly night air. It was a beautiful and peaceful night, one that made me long for some company. I could hear the wind rustling the leaves in the trees and the foraging of small nocturnal animals. They were just skunks and raccoons—no sign of anything larger.

I stood out there as long as I could, my ears tuned to the various sounds of the night, but there were no long sorrowful howls or low grunts or staccato tree knocks. Finally, the cold air drove me inside for a cup of hot herbal tea before I headed off to bed—still not a believer in Bigfoot.

☙ 11 ❧
Rigby at the Market

There were times that I wished that my phone didn't have cellular reception. Granted, it was nice to be able to keep up with my email. If I hadn't been able to log on, I would have had nearly a thousand waiting for me when I got home. Still, navigating close to 50 emails a day on a cell phone wasn't much fun. A good chunk of said emails are junk messages that don't get read and just get chucked into the trash folder. A few are inquiries about hiring me for my organizational skills and those I need to read. I need a paycheck to make my mortgage and buy food. And every once in a while, I get one that assumes I am taking the job—without any confirmation from me.

I had worked with a particular woman in the past on organizing and managing an annual spring event at the university, but it always fell in the middle of two larger projects that I always agreed to manage. Not just larger projects, but better-paying ones. I rubbed my temples as I saw my schedule that I had worked so carefully and diligently to clear off to give me some breathing room crowding back up again.

I suppose I should give this woman some credit because in the past she's more or less come to me assuming that I would work it without really asking me if I could. Each time, instead of telling her no, I cave and work it. I've always managed, some years with less hair than others, but the thought of cramming it on top of the things that I had already committed to just made my head ache and my stomach knot up. Cramming my schedule overly full was just the sort of thing that I told myself I wasn't going to do anymore.

I sent an email back, telling her that I wouldn't be able to help this year, gave her the name of someone who might be interested in the job, and spent the next two days filtering through passive-aggressive guilt trips in order to get me to capitulate. This was not how I wanted to spend my time here. I was supposed to be a writer this month, not a babysitter for people without contingency plans. I resisted the urge to put her on my junk e-mail list and sent back another polite, but firm email saying "no."

The weekend came, my next to last here in the Ozark mountains, and I was on my way to the Sanders Street Market in a nearby town. I stumbled over a flyer for it at the laundromat earlier in the week and decided it was worth checking out. It looked as if it were primarily a farmer's market during the spring and summer but, with the seasons turning and the harvest over, it turned to mostly arts and crafts.

I made my way through a quaint historic downtown towards an old square not too far north of Fayetteville and found some public parking. There was a plaque on the square, detailing the not so savory history of the square as a site for slave auctions. Suddenly, the quiet, picturesque square didn't look quite so picturesque. I swallowed against the uneasy feeling that welled up from the reminder of our not so congenial history. From the square, it was a short one-block walk to the actual market. I could see the tents of the various vendors from the lot, bold colors against a bright blue sky.

Since it had taken me almost an hour and a half to get here, I was pleased to see that the Sanders Street Market was fairly extensive. It spanned two street blocks and boasted a good crowd of shoppers today. I was half-afraid that it would be a small market without many booths. I loved farmer's markets and craft fairs and could spend a few hours browsing the booths and tasting the various foods made by small local bakeries, dairies, and food trucks.

I took my time walking along the tents, looking at the various goods that were being offered and making mental notes of which stalls I wanted to revisit. I didn't have any bags or means to carry anything that I bought, so I was hoping to find someone that sold bags. I found the organizer's stall that did sell printed canvas bags. At twenty dollars apiece, I thought they were a little expensive, but I handed over the bill nonetheless. I didn't relish the idea of juggling various packages while I walked the market.

Bag in hand, I retraced my steps and visited several of the tents that interested me. There was a woman who had handmade soaps, and I bought some as part of Christmas gifts. Someone else had some wood turned bowls, and I spent a pretty penny on one that was made with spalted wood. The warm cream-colored wood mottled with black veins was beautiful. It had been polished with what the craftsman assured me was a food grade wax. I thought it would make a nice addition to my kitchen and could picture it on my counter filled with oranges and apples.

It occurred to me while I toured the various stalls that I was feeling happy. And while I had felt lonely at times during my trip to the Ozarks, I hadn't felt the weight of the world on my shoulders lately. I wondered what the change was. Could it have been as easy as just getting away from everything? I wasn't sure, but whatever it was, I needed to hold onto it.

My favorite booth was one that sold pottery. I am completely in love with pottery have been slowly adding to my collection over the years from markets just like this one. I had a collection of brightly glazed bowls and platters of varying sizes, as well as a few bud vases. One sat on my kitchen windowsill at home, while the other rested on my bedside table.

"Hey there!" the owner, who wore a pair of dark jeans and a plaid button-down over a red t-shirt greeted me. He was into the lumberjack look, with a full beard and a head of gelled hair. He was built like one, too. I admired his broad shoulders and firm forearms and wondered for a few minutes if he were single. Not that I was looking, mind you. I didn't see any reason why I couldn't admire a well-built man when one was standing in front of me.

I smiled and said a return hello as I turned my attention to the various pieces he had to offer. A large bowl caught my eye. It was two-toned, a soft dove gray color accented with a deep red. "Do you do all of these yourself or work with a group?"

"I am the sole potter," he grinned back. He took a moment to ogle me in my monochrome skirt, t-shirt, and long, crocheted cardigan. I wondered if he thought he saw a kindred spirit. I have to admit that being ogled by him felt nice. It was good to be noticed.

"I'm Rigby," he said, sticking his hand out towards me. I shook it, giving him my name in return. As a name, Rigby fitted him, so I didn't rename him as I was wont to do with strangers (not that I told them, of course). His warm hand swallowed mine and, I could feel a little tingle run up my arm. "You from around here?"

"No, just in town for a little while," I replied. "I live one state over."

"Oh," he smiled and nodded as he spoke, but he sounded a touch disappointed. I felt a little bad although I was not sure why.

"What got you into pottery?" I asked, still admiring the bowl.

"I took a class a few years back," he said, looking towards a display of beautifully glazed bowls. "I'd always like the stuff and thought it might be something to do in my spare time." He looked back at me, his lips curving into a smile again, "It occurred to me one night that I might be able to make a living at it and I sure as hell liked it better than construction."

"It does help to do what you love," I agreed as a display of mugs caught my eye.

"I figured that you only live once, so why waste your life with anything that you don't like? I had an opportunity to get into a couple of markets, so I took the leap."

"That can be a scary leap," I said. "I did that going into business for myself a few years back and didn't sleep for close to three months afterward from all the worry."

He laughed, "That sounds familiar. It can be scary, especially while you are waiting for the money to come in, but when you see a chance, you have to take it—at least that is my philosophy."

"My biggest issue is juggling everything that people come to me to manage. I need to learn to say 'no' more often," I gave him a mildly chagrined look with a small smile.

"That is tough, too," he agreed, his gaze somewhere lower than my face when he said it. "But sometimes it is necessary to pass one thing up in order to take advantage of something else that comes along. I spent my first year struggling to make ends meet and almost gave up before I got smart about where I went to sell."

"It looks like you've figured it out," I waved a hand at the market.

"A lot of it," he gave a small laugh as his gaze went back to my face. "There are things that I am still working through, but I am making it work. I just keep looking at each opportunity that comes and make sure I take the ones that are right for me."

His gaze slipped from my face again, and I resisted the urge to cross my arms over my chest. Instead, I moved to where the mugs were displayed since I wanted to look at them, anyway.

"I love these mugs," I picked one up and turned it over in my hand.

"Those sell well," he rose from his seat and walked to where I was standing. He towered over me by nearly a foot, which was saying something because I am not short. I wondered from his frame if he played football in high school.

He watched as I selected four mugs, each a different color. I tried not to wince at the price of twenty-two dollars each, but I really, really liked them. And, I told myself as Rigby and I carried them over to the table where he had set up his register, I was supporting a local artisan.

My cell phone rang as I set the mugs I was holding down on the card table next to Rigby's chair. It is always funny when a cell phone rings in a crowd. More than a few people around me thought that it was their phone ringing. They immediately dove into their pockets or purses to pull out their phones to check them. That always amused me. I excused myself from Rigby for the moment, promising that I would be right back to pay for the mugs and answered the phone.

"Hi! I was going to text but thought it would be easier to call. It is the weekend and all, and I am not at work." The smooth and deep voice on the other end of the phone was a familiar one.

"Hi Bane," I smiled, moving out Rigby's booth and away from the general crowd.

"Where are you? Sounds a bit noisy."

"At an outdoor market. It's a farmer's market in the spring and summer, but now it is mostly craftsmen and a few people with hothouse tomatoes and greens."

"Sounds like fun, does it run every weekend?"

"I have no idea. All I know is that it is running this weekend. I thought that I would check it out."

"Fair enough," he replied. "Have found you anything interesting?"

"I was just about to buy some handmade ceramic mugs when you called."

"Ceramic mugs? Aw, are you getting me a Christmas present? You know I like coffee." Coffee was a bonding point for Bane and me. Restless couldn't abide by the stuff, but Bane loved it. He and I agreed that we both drank too much but never did anything about controlling our consumption.

"Do you want a ceramic mug for Christmas?"

"I would love any Christmas present you gave me."

"That is sweet of you to say," I turned around and eyed the display of mugs, thinking that my budget might be able to squeeze out one more twenty-two-dollar mug.

"So... will you still be in Arkansas next week?"

"I will, why?" I asked, frowning as a middle-aged man picked up one of the mugs I'd set aside to buy. I hoped he didn't think he was going to snatch them out from underneath me. I hoped Rigby wouldn't let him.

"I am going to Fayetteville tomorrow. My co-worker who was supposed to go ended up with the flu, and I am the pinch hitter."

"Seriously?" I could feel my heart take a leap, but I didn't choose to ponder why.

"I was thinking if you tell me where the cabin is, I can see how far away we'll be from each other. Maybe we could meet for dinner one night."

I gave him the address of the cabin, and he was silent for a few minutes. While he was quiet, I looked back at my mugs and was relieved to see that Rigby had directed the man to the display where the others were kept. I would have been upset if he'd sold those mugs out from under me.

"Looks like you're about an hour away. I'll have work dinners on a couple days, but I can make sure that I have a night free for you." He paused a beat, then added, "That is if you want to have dinner together."

I looked back at Rigby who was wrapping up the bowl that I had been admiring earlier for a woman. His advice about taking opportunities when they arose came back to me. I turned back to the phone.

"Bane, I'd love to meet you for dinner."

○3 12 ○

Starlight Confessions

There was a sharp knock on the door a few minutes after six on Wednesday evening. I wiped my suddenly sweaty hands on my jeans before going to answer the door. I wasn't certain why I was feeling so nervous.

Bane stood there on the porch, his eyes looking down at the mat. No doubt he was reading the worn caption that was supposed to say, "Welcome to the Ozarks," but due to weather and time eroding away some of the letters, read more like a Klingon proverb. His gaze shifted from the mat to me, then his lips quirked up in a smile.

"Hello, Zois," he said, using his online nickname for me. He handed me a bag with a bottle of Zinfandel.

"Hi," I replied, shifting out of the way to let him into the cabin.

Bane and I first met face to face during a guild retreat that we attended about a year ago. It was in Tampa, Florida, where the guild leader lived. It had been a fun weekend, getting to meet the people behind the voices I had heard on the Discord server while we negotiated raids, fractals, and guild runs.

Bane stood about six feet tall. His blond hair was just past his shoulders, and he kept it tied back with a plain band. He was an engineering consultant and for a little while, had gotten quite a bit of grief about his hair, but over time (according to him), people had come to realize that his knowledge and professional capacity wasn't adversely tied to the length of his hair.

After some discussion the previous afternoon, we had decided that we would just grill something at the cabin, rather than try to find a restaurant. So, I had made the trip into town for a pair of steaks, corn on the cob, and some lettuce and tomato for a salad. He promised to bring the wine.

"The drive up here was both gorgeous and scary," he said, taking off his coat. He looked around for a moment, then back at me, "Ah, where should I put this?"

"Back of the couch is fine. There is a coat closet here, but no free hangers," I waved a hand towards the couch and headed to the kitchen, wine in hand. "Shall I open this and pour some glasses?"

"After that drive, yes," he grinned, then looked around the cabin. "Nice place. You said it was owned by a friend of yours?"

"Yes," I said, fishing out a dubious looking corkscrew from a drawer filled with various kitchen odds and ends. "He lived in the area for a long time," I struggled to get the corkscrew into the cork, "and used the cabin for hunting and fishing. He rents it most weekends. He's living on a boat in the Keys, and mostly uses the income from the cabin rental to keep him in beer." I tried and failed to get the corkscrew started. The corkscrew was old and apparently dull. Very, very dull.

"Sounds like a way to go," Bane said, moving to the kitchen's bar and watching me struggle with the bottle.

"He seems to be enjoying it," I managed to get the corkscrew into the cork, but getting the cork out proved to be another problem. After a few moments of trying, I slid the bottle, corkscrew and all, over to him.

"How have you liked being up here by yourself?" he asked as he worked on trying to lever out the cork. I felt vindicated as he, too, struggled with it.

"I've enjoyed it here, although sometimes it gets lonely," I replied as he managed to get the cork out. I pushed two wine glasses towards him, "I've done some hiking, a lot of thinking, and wrote my book—I just need to finish a few more chapters and edit it before I make the decision to send it somewhere and hope for the best."

"I wondered if you'd get lonely," he said as he poured the wine, "you always seemed to be going somewhere and spending time with people. Not afraid to get out and live life when you could."

I watched as he poured the red liquid into the two glasses, thinking about not being afraid to live life. Was that really me? I never saw myself that way. I looked at him as he set the bottle down then handed me one of the glasses. Was that how he saw me? I never know how other people look at me and sometimes when they give me some insight into their thoughts, I feel surprised.

"You're looking dubious, Zois," he picked up the other glass and took a sip.

"I was just thinking about what you said," I replied before taking a sip from my own glass. "I don't see myself as a brave person taking life by the horns. I see myself more like trying muddle through while doing my best to look like I have my act together."

"You are one of the bravest people I know," he set his glass down and gave me a serious look. "You took a leap to go in business for yourself, even though you are an introvert. You push yourself out of your comfort zone to try new things all the time. You took a whole month off and jumped in a car to drive to the middle of the Ozarks to write a book and sort through some thoughts. That took a lot of courage."

"I never thought of it that way," I looked down into my wine glass and saw my murky reflection on the surface. It was a poor portent of my future.

"More times than I can count these past few weeks, I wished that I was able to do the same."

"Get your act together or look like it?" I teased him from over the rim of my wine glass.

"Well, yeah," he grinned back at me. "But just take off and follow a dream, even if it is a small one. Make a bucket list and do something about it."

"I have a bucket list, but I've barely made a dent in it. I figure that I have a few more years before crunch time. But, yeah...I've thought about a lot of things while I've been here. Mostly things about where I am now and what I want out of life. Not sure if I have come up with any answers." I said with a shrug.

"I like to think that you don't have to come up with the right answer all the time. Sometimes what is the right answer can change, you know?"

He had a point: the right answer could change, depending on your situation. Maybe the whole point was to have faith in what you believed in and keep going forward towards your goals. That was some food for thought.

"Oh, before I forget," I said, "I got you something."

"Really?" he grinned.

I set my wine glass down and went to the living room where I had the mug I bought him from Rigby at the Sander Street Market. It was still wrapped in newspaper and settled in the plain Kraft paper bag that Rigby had put it in. "Here you go."

"What is it?" he asked, taking the package.

"An early Christmas present? Open it and see."

He did, his eyes lighting up at the deep mahogany brown ceramic mug with a cream-colored rim and interior. It was the most masculine looking mug there, and the one that I thought he would like the best.

"I love it," he grinned at me. "I was just teasing about the Christmas present, but I will keep the mug."

I waved a hand at it, "I didn't mind getting you something to remember your short trip to the Ozarks."

"I'll use it when I get home for my morning coffee. Thank you, Zois." He set the mug on the counter and looked at me, "I wish I could have made this a longer trip with less work, but..." he shrugged.

"Coming out here has a been a great vacation. I really needed the break from everything."

"So, you're almost done with the book?"

"I am," I said, nodding my head slightly in affirmation. "I still have a chapter or two to finish it up, and then there will be the long process of editing it. But yeah, I wrote it."

"Will you let me read the book?"

I looked at him, his face earnest. "If you want, I'll email you a copy."

"I'd like that," he said softly. "And a copy when you get it published."

"There is no guarantee that a publisher will pick it up," I said with a small sigh.

"Then you can self-publish."

That was Bane, ever the cheerleader. I only wished that Restless was that supportive all the time. We stood there for a long moment, his eyes locked with mine. Suddenly, I found myself wishing that neither of us had a significant other. That Bane could spend the month out here with me in the Ozarks, hiking, exploring, and enjoying life together. I broke contact, feeling a bit chicken as I did. Bane had a girlfriend, and I had Restless. Or I thought I had Restless. More and more I was beginning to wonder what I really did have with him.

"I should start the corn on the grill if we want to eat," I said quietly, pushing away from the counter.

The grill itself was gas, so there was no waiting for charcoal to heat up. It was just turn on the burner and toss the food on. I liked that because I often decided to grill on the spur of the moment.

Bane picked up the wine glasses while I gathered up a pair of on-the-cob corn that I had buttered, salted, and wrapped in foil, and the steaks. He followed me outside into the chilly night, drifted over to the railing, and looked out over the darkened ridge. It would be too cold to eat outside, but not too cold to spend a little bit of time enjoying the clean night air.

"How long for the corn?" he asked once I joined him by the railing. He handed me my wine glass.

"Give it ten minutes then we can toss the steaks on," I said leaning against the rail.

"It sounds like you are more relaxed," he said after several long moments of companionable silence while we just sipped our wine.

I liked that, companionable silence. Of being comfortable enough with someone that you could just be together quietly without feeling the need to speak. I suppose it was the difference between sensing a closeness between two people or seeing it as a void that needed to be filled.

"I am more relaxed," I agreed. "I think it has helped that I haven't had to juggle work, being online, and my social life."

"You hinted more than once over the summer that you were feeling overwhelmed. Do you think that you just took too much on?"

I nodded. "Yeah. Far too much. While I've been here, I made some decisions to cut back on work projects. I need to be a little smarter and more organized about what I take and grow a backbone when someone wants me to take on something that I don't have time for."

"I think your backbone is just fine," he leaned backward to peer at my back.

"No, it isn't. Not really. But I am resolved to do better. Aside from being smarter about the jobs I take for work, I also need to think about how much time I am spending online."

"Oh, really?" there was a slight wary note in his voice. After all, most of the time we spent together was online.

"I play too many games and try to be involved in the guilds that I participate in. I could spend hours every night doing something in-game, and it still is not enough to keep up with everything. I need to cut back. I realized while I was here and able to get outside and hike that I haven't been as active as I had in the past—before I got involved in online games."

"I see. What games would you give up?"

"I don't know yet," I let out a long sigh. "I'll probably give up all but one or two games and cut back on running dungeons and raids in the ones that I stay in. I've gained ten pounds from just sitting in my desk chair playing video games, and I have to juggle going out to dinner with friends with being online to participate in a raid. That doesn't seem right to me. I can't help but think that I am missing too much by spending so much time on the computer."

"I didn't know all that," he said quietly. "Or maybe I just didn't want to consider it. If you are really that tied up over it and think you need to spend less time online, then you should spend less time online." He paused a moment before asking, "Ah, would you give up the game we play together in?"

I considered his question. Whatever games I gave up, I would be saying goodbye to the friends that I had there. That thought was depressing, but I knew that I had to do something about the time I spent online to help me get back control over how I spent my time. I could hear one of my raid leaders yelling at me now for not being a team player when I told him I was leaving. I would happily give him a piece of my mind if that happened, I decided. However, the game Bane and I played in was one that I knew I would keep—it might be the only one I kept. It didn't have a monthly subscription fee, and it made more sense to give up a game I had to pay for each month rather than one I didn't.

It was also a game I didn't share with Restless, and I wondered what that said about my position concerning our relationship. That was something I would think about later.

"No, I think I'll keep our game," I smiled up at him before I moved to put the steaks on the grill and he turned to face the ridge.

We lapsed into another companionable silence. The sky was clear and filled with stars. The wind blew past softly, giving our cheeks a chilly caress and rattled the leaves in the trees. Somewhere off to my left in the underbrush, a small nocturnal animal— probably a raccoon or a skunk—was foraging.

"This looks like it would be a great view in the daylight," he finally said. "I can't say I see much out here at night, but it is peaceful. I can see why you like it here."

"Mornings out here are beautiful. The fog hangs in the air, and everything is quiet. It can get a little lonely, though."

"That does sound beautiful," he said, his gaze shifted from the trees to me. "Is that an invitation to stay the night?"

I had almost taken a sip of wine when said that, and I am glad I hadn't. I probably would have choked on it. I lowered the wine glass and looked up at him.

"I know, you are still seeing Restless," he sighed out, sounding a bit bitter to my ears. He turned back around and resumed leaning on the railing.

"I am," I replied gently, "although I've done a lot of thinking about that. Thinking about what I want and all the little points you've made about our relationship. Regardless, I don't think your girlfriend would like that idea."

He drew in a deep breath and let it out in a long sigh. "She and I are no longer dating. Haven't been for close to four months."

"Seriously? What happened? You seemed to really like her." This was surprising news because he hadn't said a word about breaking up. Of course, now that I thought about it, he hadn't mentioned her in a while, and I hadn't asked about her.

"We didn't work out," he continued looking at me as if I was going to give him the answer to a question he'd yet to ask. "I realized that there was someone else I wanted to be with, someone else who made me laugh. Someone I clicked with."

I swallowed as I looked up at him, wondering just where he was going with this and how I felt about it.

He took a deep breath and continued, "It occurred to me that the only reason you and I are not here spending time together for the past month is that for the past three years we've known each other, either you've been involved with someone, or I have been."

"True," I said softly.

"I don't want to tell you who you should get involved with, and if it is really love you are feeling with Restless, I don't want to get in the way of that, but Zois... he's part of the reason why you've been so depressed lately. In the last six months, you've been together, he's stood you up more and more. He's made no move to further your relationship and wasn't it you who told me that with him, you often felt like Plan B?"

"I know," I sighed and closed my eyes.

"I've been looking in from the outside on this thing and it looks to me that the whole thing fell apart a long time ago," he said gently. "I have to tell you that it looks like you are holding onto a ghost."

"It feels that way," I whispered. I didn't feel sad, just resigned.

He let out a short bark of laughter, "Hell, this isn't the conversation I thought we'd have tonight. But Zois, honey, it hurts me to see him twist you in knots. He throws enough attention your way to keep you around when it suits him. I keep thinking that I'm the one you lean on, I'm the person you turn to when he hurts you, so why I am not the one you want to trade erotic texts with?"

That made me laugh, not unkindly, and he joined me.

"I think you said it before," I put my hand over his once our laughter abated, "our timing has been off." I gave it a light squeeze. He turned his hand and wrapped his fingers around mine before I could remove it. His hand was warm against the chilly night air and set off the butterflies in my stomach.

"I am not going to ask to stay the night, but while you are up here thinking about life and where you want to be, promise me you'll think about him and if he and his disregard for you are what you want in a lover. Is he the one you'll love forever?"

My eyes caught his, and I felt something tremble inside me. Something that had nothing to do with Restless and everything to do with Bane.

Feeling like a coward, I broke eye contact and looked back out into the darkness, my mind mingling all the let downs I had had with Restless over the past few months with Bane's words. I had spent a good deal of time thinking about Restless and how many times I'd felt sidelined by him. Whether or not I still loved him—or ever loved him—was a question that I needed to ask myself.

"I've been thinking about it," I said, our fingers still entwined. "Trying to make a decision, to get some courage to make a decision. It is easy to stay with the status quo."

"It can take a lot of courage to let something go. I'll be here for whatever you choose," he said, setting his wine glass on the railing and brushing some of my hair back from my face. "If you leave him and want to take a break from men for a while, I'll still be here. And if you find yourself ready to try again, I'll still be here."

His words stayed with me through dinner and lighter topics. They continued to swirl in my head as I lay down to bed and there mingled with Rigby's words on taking opportunities when they came. I didn't get to sleep until very late that night. But I did make a few decisions.

෬ 13 ෨
Reflection on the Ridge

The next morning, I was sitting on the back deck in what I now considered my Adirondack chair with a cup of coffee warming my hand. The early morning fog curled around me and the trunks of the trees like a ghostly lover as the rising sun illuminated the sky, turning it a soft, hazy purple. I had only a few days left in my mountain sojourn before I returned to my home state and picked up life where I left off.

I was feeling surprisingly content. I thought that after Bane had told me that he wanted a deeper relationship, I would feel a myriad of emotions, each fighting one another for dominance. I wasn't sure how I felt about Bane's confession Wednesday night, but I knew that he was right about one thing: he was the person I always turned to when Restless brought me down. Bane had checked in every day with me while I was here. Sometimes we'd talk for a little while and other times it was just a text or two. It was far more than I had gotten from Restless.

I checked the time on my phone. Bane was probably at the airport, waiting to board his flight home. He told me he'd text me when he got to his apartment in upstate New York, and I didn't doubt his word. If he said he'd do something, he would do it, and if something happened that he couldn't keep whatever promise that he made, he would tell you. It was part his personality and part the engineer in him.

I didn't know if I wanted another online relationship, and I didn't know if I should end things with Restless. I had been on the edge of saying goodbye to him more than once in the past two months, but each time I backed down. Each time things got a little better for a week or so before they grew apart again. What I did know was like the fog that was creeping across the ridgeline, my thoughts on what I should do were murky.

I finally decided that I needed to reach out to him and talk about what was going through my head. I didn't need to break things off before talking to him about what he was thinking and feeling. Without telling him what I was thinking and feeling. Our relationship deserved at least that.

I went inside to wash my coffee cup and breakfast dishes. I picked up my phone after I finished my dishes, thinking that I should make good on my thought to talk to Restless about what I was feeling. He wouldn't be awake just yet, but at least the text would be waiting for him when he did finally make it out of bed.

Hey there! Do you have some time to talk today? I hit send and watched as my phone struggled to push the text through the weak cellular signal.

There was no answer to my text when I got out of the shower, but I wasn't expecting anything until lunchtime. I returned outside and finished the last chapter of my book. A few hours later, I went back inside to eat lunch and, yes, check my messages on my phone again. Still nothing from Restless and I wondered what he was doing. There was a chance that he was busy with something and hadn't been able to get to his texts. There was also the chance that he saw it but was too engrossed in one of his online games to spend the two minutes it would take to send me a reply. Or that he didn't feel like reaching out to me.

I puttered around the cabin for another half an hour while I waited to see if Restless was going to send anything back today. Waiting around for him finally to deign to answer my text was only making me upset. My time here in the mountains was dwindling, and I didn't need to spend what little I had left inside moping about because my boyfriend wouldn't text me. I decided that I would head back to Whitaker Point Trailhead this afternoon and hike the entire loop.

The morning fog had burned off to reveal a bright and crisp day. The chill of fall was definitely in the air, and it felt like perfect hiking weather. Other people thought so, too. There were four cars in the pull-off when I arrived, and as I slipped into the fifth space, the car behind me took up the final spot in the small, six-car pull-off.

The first time I hiked this trail, the tall trees that lined the path were still mostly green, but now their foliage was a rich blanket of reds, oranges, and yellows. The sky was a perfect azure blue with a few large, fluffy clouds drifting lazily. As I stepped towards the trailhead, I thought that I was a lucky person to be able to spend such a splendid afternoon hiking in a beautiful forest. I vowed once again that when I got home, I would take more time to get out and enjoy nature.

I let my mind flow as I walked along the packed dirt trail. I am never certain where my mind will lead me when I let it wander, but I follow it wherever it goes. Now as I made my way up the ridge, it went back to Restless and my relationship with him. I wasn't surprised. My relationship with him and what I needed to do about it was foremost in my mind today.

It occurred to me that part of the problem was that when he didn't show up for one of our regular days or didn't respond to something that I sent, I never asked him why or told him that it bothered me. Occasionally, he would give me an excuse, and I would just accept it, but I never spoke up about my feelings. I told myself it was because I didn't want to seem like I was nagging him, but a part of me wondered if I didn't want to hear the answer to why he was absent. *Assuming that he'd tell me the truth*, a dark voice in my head added. He had lied to me a few times, but I had never called him on it. I wasn't certain if I saw the point.

As much as I told myself at the time that I was fine with the absenteeism, I wasn't. A piece of me realized that I had withdrawn from the relationship some over the last couple of months. Each time he missed getting online with me, I got upset and withdrew just a little bit more. That hadn't helped matters either, I thought glumly. It was as if I was drawing a shell around me to protect myself from what felt like an inevitable break-up—except the break-up hadn't occurred.

I walked on, moving to one side as I passed a pair of women coming in the opposite direction on the trail. They both sported bright knit caps on their heads and each had her hair pulled back in a pony's tail. We waved a polite hello to each other as we passed. Not long after, I reached the top of the ridge and stopped to look out over the colorful tree canopy below me. It was absolutely stunning, and for a long moment I simply stood there and stared out over the perfect view in awe.

Admitting that I bore some fault in our relationship faltering was hard for me to take. As much as I wanted to be able to say that I took the high road and all the problems that I was having were solely because of his lack of communication, I could not. I could have communicated better, too. Maybe if I had, we'd be standing here together, or maybe I would have realized that our relationship was over months ago and I wouldn't be fretting over it.

I could not put my finger on where things started to separate for the two of us. I just knew that one afternoon I realized we hadn't spent more than a day together over a two-week period. I had been sitting at my desk waiting for him to tell me when he had woken up when that little thought occurred to me. It became more and more frequent until we ended up where we were today.

I let out a long sigh and ran a hand over my face as I let that sink in. I had been waiting for Restless to make the move to communicate with me, but how much had I done on my end? Instead, I had slowly withdrawn, and most likely that had abetted his behavior. I had thought that I was being supportive, even when I was silently upset. And I hadn't said a word to him about it.

That did not change the fact that I felt like Plan B to him. Oh, he still talked sweetly to me and used endearments, but now I wondered if he just did that to keep me around. I didn't know if he was seeing someone else online or not, and I wasn't certain if that thought upset me. That fact that I had to think about my feelings on the matter bore some scrutiny.

I started down the opposite side of the ridge, heading for Whitaker Point. I passed another set of hikers, this time three older gentlemen, on the way. I rattled over my quandary with Restless without a solution for another mile before my mind decided that it wanted to turn to my job situation.

I had gotten confirmation that the project I left when I came here had finally finished. The new project lead had burned the midnight oil to get it done. It was two weeks late, but that was not my fault. It at least was on budget. I had been assured that I could get the job again next year, which was a huge sigh of relief for me. That project had paid well.

What would pay even better was the job offer in Nashville. The paperwork for the official offer would be waiting for me at the post office in my hold mail pile, but I had received the verbal offer over the phone. I like Nashville, I do, but all my friends were in Knoxville. I wasn't sure if I wanted to leave the people who meant so much to me behind, only to see a few times a year. I hadn't been prepared for how much I had missed my friends while I had been here in the Ozarks. I thought that missing them would be magnified ten-fold if I moved to another city three hours away.

The lure of a steady paycheck still dangled in front of me. A nice, steady paycheck that rolled into my bank account every two weeks. But, in order to get that stability, I would be giving up the business that I had built over the past two years. A part of me wanted to hold onto what I had built and a part of me, who had been through some lean times as a self-employed project manager, said take the job. I wouldn't have to work to find leads or always be fretting when I lost a job to someone else about being able to pay my bills and feed myself.

I reached the other trailhead at Whitaker Point as I weighed the pros and cons of the job in Nashville. I had left the corporate life because the job that I had been in didn't have the best corporate culture and that left a sour taste in my mouth. But, there was nothing to say that this company would be the same. It also helped that project management was an up and coming field, and many companies wanted to work with one, but not keep one on the payroll. I fit that niche nicely.

My hike back to my car was filled with thoughts of my friends from home, and I wondered what had transpired while I was away. I had gotten texts and emails from them as they checked in on me. A few were talking about some upcoming community events, including a Winter Fair that would showcase handmade goods that was coming up the first weekend in December. There was word that one of my favorite bands was coming to town in a few months and plans were being made for a group of us to go. I couldn't help but think that if I took the job in Nashville, there would be things, like going to a concert with my friends or trolling a craft fair one weekend with them, wouldn't happen often.

My evening was spent reading the various chapters of the book I had written, thinking about how the whole thing flowed. Overall, I was pleased with it, and I was proud of myself for setting a goal to write a book and actually finishing it. I had no idea of how good it was, but good or bad, the accomplishment remained. I now needed to decide if I was going to publish the book myself or try to submit it to a publisher. It was not a decision that I would make tonight, I thought with a yawn.

It was late, and I was sitting in bed reading *Big Sur* under a thick layer of blankets when my phone trilled, telling me I had a text. I had been reading for well over an hour, thinking that I ought to click off the light and try to get some sleep, but my brain refused to shut down. I had hoped that reading *Big Sur* would help quiet it down. I picked up my phone and out of habit, checked to see if I had something from Restless first. There was still nothing. I wasn't surprised, just stoic.

The text I received was from Bane telling me he was finally home. *I'm in,* he had typed. *Plane was delayed leaving Arkansas and then again in Cincinnati. I am beat. I enjoyed having dinner with you.*

Happy to hear that the plane didn't crash! I replied. *Did you have a good flight?*

I am happy that the plane didn't crash, too, he replied. *Flight was good. I didn't wake you, did I?*

No, just up reading, I assured him. If it hadn't been so late or if he hadn't had such a long day, I might have added that I was trying to quiet my brain from the various thoughts that had been tumbling through it all day. But it was late, and he had had a long day, and I didn't want him to feel obliged to stay up and talk to me.

Reading your book? Did you get it finished?

I did finish my book, but I am reading Big Sur *by Kerouac,* I typed back.

I'd love a copy of your book. I'll buy one when you get it published.

You sound confident that I will publish it.

I have faith that you will. And if you don't publish it, he texted, *I still would like to read it.*

I think I can manage that, I replied.

But if you do publish it, I get a signed copy.

Deal. If you are willing to buy a book, the least I can do is sign it.

I'll let you get back to reading. I am tired and am going to crash. Have a good night, Zois. He signed off.

I read over his texts again, thinking about how he kept his promise that he wouldn't pressure me to make a decision about him. That we could just be friends. That meant more to me than he would know. I texted a *Good night and sleep well* to him before going back to my book and realized that even though Restless hadn't responded to my text, I was in a good mood after hearing from Bane.

☙ 14 ❧
Big Shoal Creek

I finally finished *Big Sur.* I wasn't certain how satisfied I was with the ending, but there was some measure of hope in there. It seemed that all pieces that held the protagonist together simply unraveled to culminate in his breakdown and then the next day, he woke up completely sober with a new view on life: everything was going to be okay. I went to sleep that night thinking about the series of alcohol driven choices he had made and how he tried to retrace his steps and find his path. He fell and fell hard, but instead of staying down, he got back up and kept going. There was something to be admired about that, even though the ending seemed pat.

Friday afternoon found me at Big Shoal Creek with the late October sun was shining brightly. There was a small chill in the air, making a jacket necessary but it wasn't unpleasant. The trees were brilliant in color, their dark brown trunks topped with orange, red, and gold and the ground was becoming dotted with falling leaves. It made me think of the carpet lining the halls of some grand hotel.

I had taken one last hike, a two-mile loop that was an easy trail. It didn't have any steep inclines or crest over a ridge but wound its way quietly through the trees. There were several markers on the ground, making notes of various types of trees or talking about flowers. Not that there were any flowers at this time of the year. I thought that this might be a pretty trail in the spring when the flowers were in bloom.

There were quite a few people out today, taking advantage of the brilliant fall day. They were bundled up in coats and gathered in groups of friends talking happily to each other. I listened to the distant chatter but didn't focus on any one conversation. In a few months that would be me, with my friends, when we went camping in the spring. I promised myself I would make time to go.

The Ozarks were my Bixby Canyon, or at least that was what I thought. Some grand and beautiful place to think and plot and map my place in my life and my world. I was here at Big Shoal Creek to review the past month of reading, writing, hiking, and revelations. It seemed a much grander idea when I drove over here. As if I might commune with some spirits and receive some insight to all my questions and a set of trail markers for my journey through life.

Now, it was just me sitting on the ground watching the creek while letting my mind flow from one thought to the next. There were no spirits to guide me or trail markers to show me my path. Just a collection of thoughts and realizations and a sense of serenity that I did not have before. I consoled myself with the knowledge that I was not going to have an alcohol-induced breakdown and I had finally made some much-needed decisions.

I was not going to take the job in Nashville. A piece of me told myself that that was a foolish thing to do, but my home and friends were in Knoxville and after spending a month here in the Ozarks, I knew wouldn't be happy moving away. While a part of me knew that some of the weight that I had been feeling was from my job, I didn't need to jump ship at the first opportunity. I just needed to manage my time better and get a get a firmer backbone to tell people that I couldn't take on their project. That would be something that would take practice, but it was something that I told myself I would learn to do.

I had also made the decision of which games I was going to stop playing and what forums I was going to leave. I needed to reduce my online presence to have time to myself and get back to all the things that I used to do but no longer had time for. I had spent part of the morning writing up an explanation as to why I was leaving. At first, it had been something lengthy and filled with apologies, but after reading it, I discarded it for something far simpler. I would put it on the various forums when I got home, and then hop into the games to say goodbye in person before I shut them off.

Getting used to not being on the computer and getting myself back in the habit of getting out and being active would take some time, but I had a few friends who I knew would be more than happy to drag my rear out of the house each weekend if I just asked them to.

Another realization that I came to was that it was time to end things with Restless. I should have ended it months ago when he started missing more and more of our get-togethers. The excuses he gave me were often weak, or none at all, and more than a few times I know that he flat out lied to me. No, I hadn't called him on any of it, and that was on me, but that didn't absolve him of his part in all it. We hadn't had much of a relationship for the past few months, so there was no need to keep pretending that something was there.

I wasn't certain what kept me from breaking it off before. Perhaps it was just my optimism that kept me believing that I had something when really I didn't.

I thought about all the small clues of disinterest there had been over the last six months and wondered why I had been too blind to see them. I thought of how many times I had been upset and disappointed and how that eventually dwindled down to acceptance and resignation.

As I sat there watching the water, I could see how the whole relationship had become one-sided. That he had moved on without telling me and I had become Plan B: the person he went to where there wasn't anyone else available. I didn't need to waste time with a relationship where I was only wanted because there wasn't a better offer on the table. I had wasted too much time on him already.

I thought that there might be tears with the decision. That I might waver and hurriedly grab my phone to see if there had been any messages from him. But I knew that there wouldn't be anything. He hadn't responded to the text I sent Thursday. In fact, there hadn't been a peep from him at all for over a week, even on the days that we normally met. There might not be any tears, but there was a sense of resolve and finality with a hint of sadness. What I felt might not have been love, but I had liked the man.

I thought about what I wanted from a relationship. There had been a disconnection in having a relationship being solely online, and I had to ask myself if I wanted to try another online relationship again. There were some that worked, I had at least two friends meet their significant others online, and things were working out well for them. But then I had friends in town in relationships with someone who lived close to them. Someone, they could go out to dinner with and kiss goodnight. People who were around to visit the park and spend the night or sit next to at a movie. They always seemed more in tune with each other than I ever felt with Restless.

My thoughts shifted to Bane and his visit to me way out here in the Ozarks. It had been a fluke—his co-worker getting sick which necessitated him coming to the area. But he had come, and he had made it a point to see me. The evening was spent talking about the area and what I had done. He was interested in the hiking opportunities and the Sanders Street Market. Our evening together made me realized that I had more in common with him than I did Restless.

"If you need another mountain escape," Bane had said, "or just want a quiet weekend away, let me know. I'd love to spend some time with you away from computers and work. Maybe not out here, but the Smokys or the Adirondacks."

I thought about those words as I scooped up a flat, round river stone. It was dark gray, almost black, with white flecks of mica in it.

Bane had told me that he would be waiting. He would give me space and time and be there when I was ready. In some ways, he had been more of boyfriend to me than Restless had, minus the intimate parts. He had been there to bolster me, jolly me out of pensive moods, and cheer my victories. But he would be another online relationship, and after Restless, I was not sure if I would be satisfied with that.

The ability to be face to face with someone. To be close enough to touch them. That was a much stronger glue keeping two people together than just words over a Skype channel. I was a bit jealous of my friends who had that, I realized. Jealous that they could snuggle on the couch with someone to watch a movie, while I had to do it long distance over the internet, with only a keyboard to express emotions and actions.

Did I want someone that I could actually kiss goodnight after a date? Someone close enough for to me touch without emotes. It was something that I would need to think about over the next few weeks.

What I did know was that I was not going to jump into another relationship right away.

At least the tug-of-war over my organizational skills was over. After several long and frustrating days of saying I wouldn't be able to take on any new projects, even if I had worked on them in the past, I had gone over the woman's head. It was quite possible that the move cost me jobs from her in the future, but her attitude about the whole situation grated on me. It was like I had a vacuum salesman in my house who wouldn't leave unless I bought the vacuum—or called the police to evict him.

A glint of orange across the water caught my eye, and I looked up to see the sun starting to sink the in the sky. I hadn't meant to stay quite this long as I didn't want to drive up the mountain with all the narrow and steep switchbacks in the dark. I let out a long sigh, wishing that I had a few more hours out here to rattle through all the thoughts in my head.

"And then it started getting dark, I trudged back to where the car was parked. No closer to any kind of truth, as I must assume was the same with you."

The final strains of Death Cab for Cutie's song, *Bixby Canyon Bridge*, floated through my mind. I would always have questions, always be looking forward and wondering if there was a better way to get to where I wanted to go. And if the last few months had been any indication, where I wanted to go would change over time. There wasn't any single, great answer to my questions, only quiet realizations that the occasional wrong turn was going to happen and was okay. Sometimes that wrong turn was exactly what you needed, and if not, you could backtrack and take the right path.

I let the river stone I had been holding fall out of my hand. It hit the bank with a dull thud. Giving the rushing water one last look, I turned and made my way back to my car, pondering the truth that I reached.

☙ 15 ☜
Goodbye at Sunrise

Life was always changing. It wasn't about picking one direction and sticking with it but taking the direction that was right for you at the time. You might find yourself a mile or so down the road and realize that you need to turn around and go back. That was me, here in the Ozarks. I had gone down a wrong road and came here to turn around and head back. Find a new road to travel for a while.

Life was also full of surprises. Some were the bright, merry kind, that lifted your heart and made you laugh. Some were dismal and shocking, turning your stomach to knots with the thought. Others were born from assumptions that at one time seemed valid, but you never thought to challenge or change over time. You just put blinders on and kept on going, until one day something ripped the blinders off and forced you to confront the idea that maybe your assumption wasn't what it was at all.

And, if occasionally, a fetid and haggard undead corpse rises up to eat whatever unicorn was gracing you with good fortune, you ride out the bad times with a focus on the future and look for your next opportunity.

My final morning came, and I took my coffee out on the back porch as had been my habit for the last month. The sun had yet to make its appearance, but the lightening of the night sky with shades of violet and red promised that it would rise soon. I settled into my Adirondack chair and sipped my coffee with the fog-shrouded trees and shivered a little in the chilly mountain air. There had been a noticeable drop in temperature over the time I had been here, a sign that October was nearly over, and the holidays would begin soon. The peace and quiet of the morning settled into my being, preparing me for the long drive home. I might be traveling the same route I had when coming, but mentally the roads were vastly different.

I relaxed in my Adirondack chair and thought about my month here. It was hard to believe that it was over and while there were times that the days seemed to drag by, it suddenly seemed like I had just got here. One thing I did know was that with each decision to let something go, my stress level eased. For the first time in many months, I was feeling happy. I hadn't realized how much of a burden I had felt with trying to juggle numerous online games while keeping up with my job. In trying to race ahead, I had inadvertently set myself up to fall. I also hadn't realized how much of my unhappiness had stemmed from Restless.

After coming home from Big Shoal Creek, I had sent an email to Restless telling him that I wanted to break things off. I would have called him, but the weak cellular signal liked to drop calls. I wasn't mean or angry, in fact, I tried very hard to keep it neutral and a touch friendly. I did not want it to seem like I was attacking him. I just told him that it seemed like things had cooled between us and how we were spending less and less time together and how it looked like it was time that we both moved on. I wished him well at the end of it, and I really did mean it. That was two days ago, and he had had plenty of time to get the email, but I hadn't gotten any response from him. I checked my email again as I made coffee this morning and watched as the various messages filed in on my phone. A few requests for work, quite a bit of junk, more book suggestions from Amazon, and nothing from Restless.

I thought that after over year of being together, of him telling me that he loved me, that he would have something to say with my breaking it off. He would at least send something back saying goodbye, and if he was really serious about having our relationship work, find a way to stay together. At the very least acknowledge the message. But there was nothing.

That told me all I needed to know about our relationship.

I sipped my coffee and was aware that I felt oddly detached from it. Somewhere between Big Shoal Creek when I had made the decision to call it quits with him, and now, I had accepted that I needed to move on. That whatever had been between us wasn't strong enough to last. I also came to realize that our relationship had been over months ago, but I was too stubborn to realize it.

My time here in the mountains had been a much-needed break from my frenzied schedule, and while I was feeling a little homesick, a part of me would miss this place. Miss the quiet mornings on the porch with the fog and the majestic view of the ridge. I would miss the easy access to hiking trails and the clean, fresh mountain air. However, I wouldn't miss the switchbacks or the laundromat.

I thought about the few people that I had met—Harry the Sasquatch Hunter and Rigby the Potter—and how their little bits of wisdom on life and never losing hope had inspired me. I wasn't sure if such tidbits of insight would have had the same impact coming from one of my friends. Perhaps I just needed the opinions of a stranger who didn't know me or my troubles and wasn't tailoring words to jolly me out of a mood.

I thought about the other people whose paths that I had crossed—from Skeptical Mug O' Beer Man to Cross Crew Cut Laundry Guy to Bored Waitress. Maybe my next book would be based on the people that I saw here. Sure, I wouldn't base the characters on anything more than my impressions of them, but there might be a fun and quirky story in all of it.

And maybe I'd take some time off to head to a cabin in the mountains to write it.

I went inside to refill my coffee mug and get breakfast when my phone rang. It was still laying beside the coffee pot where I had left it while I took my coffee on the porch. I told myself that whatever texts or emails that were on the phone could wait an hour while I simply enjoyed my last morning with the fog, trees, and ridge, and took a little time for myself. I picked the phone up and felt my heart leap. Bane was calling. It was quarter of six in the morning, and he was calling.

"Just checking in before you start your drive," he said without preamble. His smooth voice washed over me, inciting memories of chatting on the back deck and having dinner with him.

"I am almost ready to go," I replied. "The cabin is clean, my bags are packed, and all I need to do is empty the coffee pot and take out the kitchen garbage when I am ready to head out. Let's hope I manage to make it down the mountain without sliding off into a ravine."

He laughed, "I'll call you tonight and make certain I don't have to get a tow truck to pull you out."

"I appreciate that," I said softly. We were silent for a small moment before I spoke again, "I called it off."

"What?" he sounded a bit confused.

"With Restless. I sent him an email calling it quits. Told him that I thought we needed to move on."

"What did he say?"

"Take a guess."

Bane was quiet for a moment. "He didn't say anything, did he?"

"Nope, not a single thing came back. Not even an acknowledge or a goodbye."

"You are better off without him," Bane told me gently. It wasn't the first time he had told me that. I had lost count of the number of times he had said those words to me. "My offer still stands... when you think you are ready."

"I'll be honest here, Bane, after spending six months being mostly ignored in an online relationship, I am not certain want my next relationship to be online."

"That is something we'd have to work through," he said, although I thought I heard a sigh in his voice. "But we're online friends. Do you feel like I am ignoring you?"

"No," I said quickly, shaking my head even though I knew he couldn't see me. "You've spent more time chatting with me than he has."

"That won't change if our relationship does, you know."

"I know... but it is still an online relationship. I want something tangible. Someone to go out to dinner with, head to a fair, hike a trail, cuddle with on the couch."

"I want those things, too."

"We live over seven hundred miles apart."

"For now, but if a relationship is worth something, then you figure those things out. I promise I would make an effort to see you. Take trips and do those things. When I have a vacation to take, I would take it with you. And if things work out between us, compromise and move to the same town," he sounded earnest, his voice speeding up as he spoke.

It was more than Restless had been willing to do. I leaned back against the kitchen counter and stared out the sliding glass doors to the back deck wondering how I managed to spend six months of my life with someone who barely spoke to me.

I must have been silent for too long because when Bane spoke again, his voice was soft and a little resigned, "I know you probably want some time off from relationships, and I don't mean to push, but I want you to know where I stand. I'll still be here when you are ready to make that leap. Until then, things can be status quo with us."

My lips quirked in a smile. "You were always good at lifting my spirits."

"You always lift mine, so the least that I can do is return the favor. If I was having a bad day, I knew that I could reach out to you and you would cheer me up."

"I didn't know that," I said softly. I had no idea that I had been his Wonderwall. Something warm bloomed in my chest with that thought.

We said goodbye a few moments later, with him promising me that he'd call this evening. I didn't wonder if he would or not. Bane always kept his promises. Perhaps in a few months, I would take him up on his offer for a deeper relationship than just friends but, for now, I simply wanted to get used to my new road.

Speaking of roads, I needed to get moving on the one that would lead me home. If I got enough miles in today, I'd be home in time for a Halloween party a friend of mine throwing tomorrow night. My car was packed and waiting, as was the road before me. I finished the few tasks that were left and then took a moment to walk through the various rooms of the small cabin, and then walked outside to the back deck and breathed in the mountain air one last time.

The fog still hung lazily about the trees, caressing the trunks in a slow and ancient dance. It was only six-thirty, and it would be a while yet before the sun was able to burn it off, but it was sparse. I felt that I could take the risk on driving down the mountain early on a Sunday morning. The birds chattered noisily in the waxing dawn, and the leaves whispered invitingly as the wind drifted past. I felt a small pang of melancholy in my heart and I knew would miss this place.

"Goodbye cabin and goodbye mountains," I said as I looked out over the ravine, committing the fog-shrouded trees to memory. Perhaps the next time I came here, it would be with Bane.

I drew in a deep breath and let it out slowly, "Goodbye, Restless."

I turned and walked from the back deck, through the cabin, and to my car, taking the time to make certain that all the windows and doors were locked tight. I paused after I opened the car door and looked up at the painted sky, which was now in the full bloom of the sunrise.

"The mountains called and I came."

About the Author

Kate Cavett is fond of coffee, hiking, and foggy mountain mornings. Kate lives in Tennessee, in the shadow of the Great Smoky Mountains.

www.ingramcontent.com/pod-product-compliance
Lightning Source LLC
Chambersburg PA
CBHW020412150626
46554CB00013B/788